Ajit Narayan is a professional freelance cartoonist who has been drawing for reputed publishing houses and other print media for over 20 years. As a workshop consultant for Scholastic India, he conducts cartoon workshops in schools within and outside Delhi. He is also the author of the books *Cartooning with Ajit Narayan* and *How to Draw Cartoon Animals*.

This edition is dedicated to my
wife **Liji** & daughter **Alankrita**

Published by Scholastic India Pvt. Ltd.
A subsidiary of Scholastic Inc., New York, 10012 (USA).
Publishers since 1920, with international operations in Canada,
Australia, New Zealand, the United Kingdom, India, and Hong Kong.

For information regarding permission, write to:
Scholastic India Pvt. Ltd.
A-27, Ground Floor, Bharti Sigma Centre,
Infocity-I, Sector-34, Gurgaon 122001 (India).

First edition: April 2012
Reprint: July; September; November 2012; January; May; August
2013; April; May; August; September 2014; June 2015; February 2016
; August; December 2018, 2022
ISBN-13: 978-81-8477-855-7

Printed at Shivam Offset Press, New Delhi

Draw Cartoons With

AJIT NARAYAN

SCHOLASTIC
New York Toronto London Auckland
Sydney New Delhi Hong Kong

Written and illustrated by Ajit Narayan

CONTENTS

CONTENTS

COMIC HEAD

When you are drawing a comic head for the first time, begin with a circle. Later, you can get more adventurous with head shapes.

Start with the basic shape of the head, for example, a circle. Draw two guidelines through the circle.

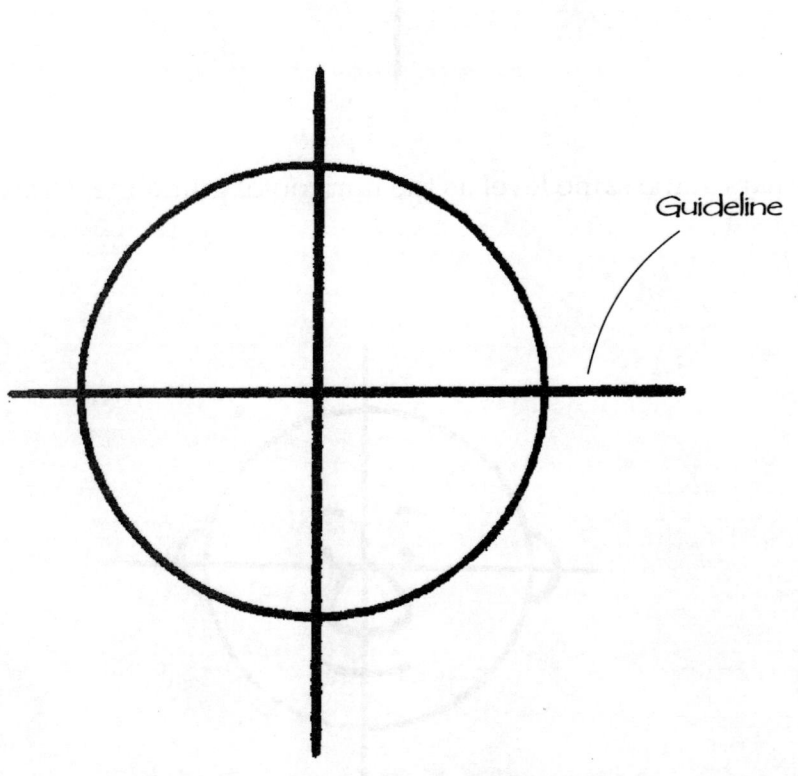

Guideline

Draw the bridge of the nose at the point where the two guidelines meet. The eyes rest on top of the horizontal line and the eyebrows above them.

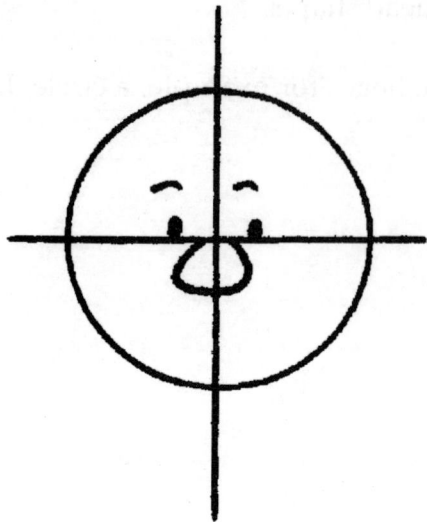

Add the ears at the same level as the horizontal guideline. Draw a mouth below the nose.

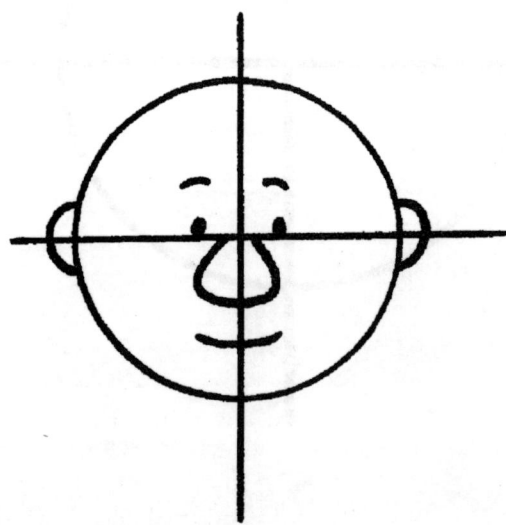

Now, erase your guidelines and fill in the details such as hair, dimple, creases or chin.

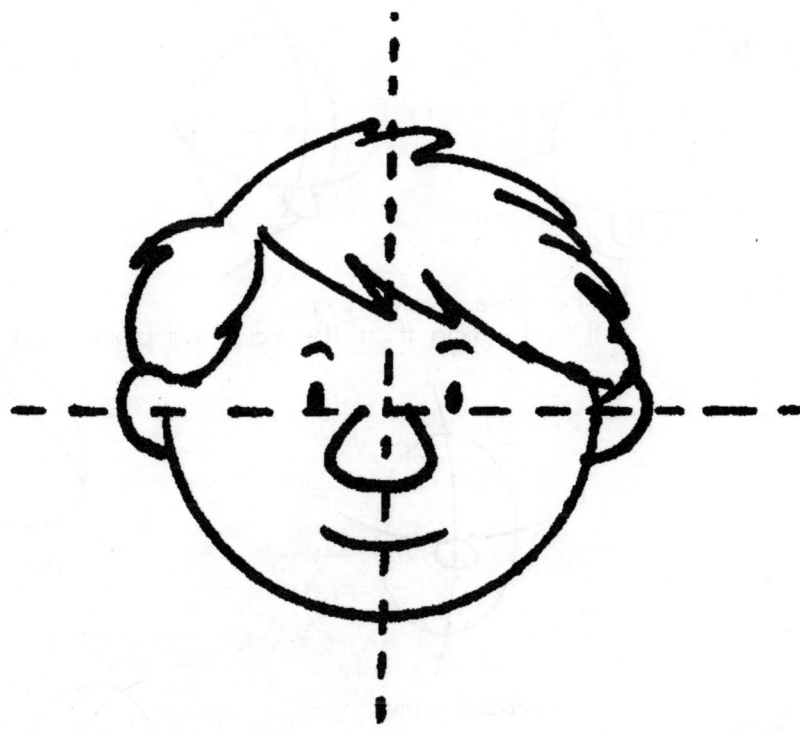

Tip: It is possible to reposition various facial features to achieve different effects.

ROTATING HEADS

We need to learn how to rotate the head in all directions while making sure that it always looks like the same character.

Practise and copy these positions.

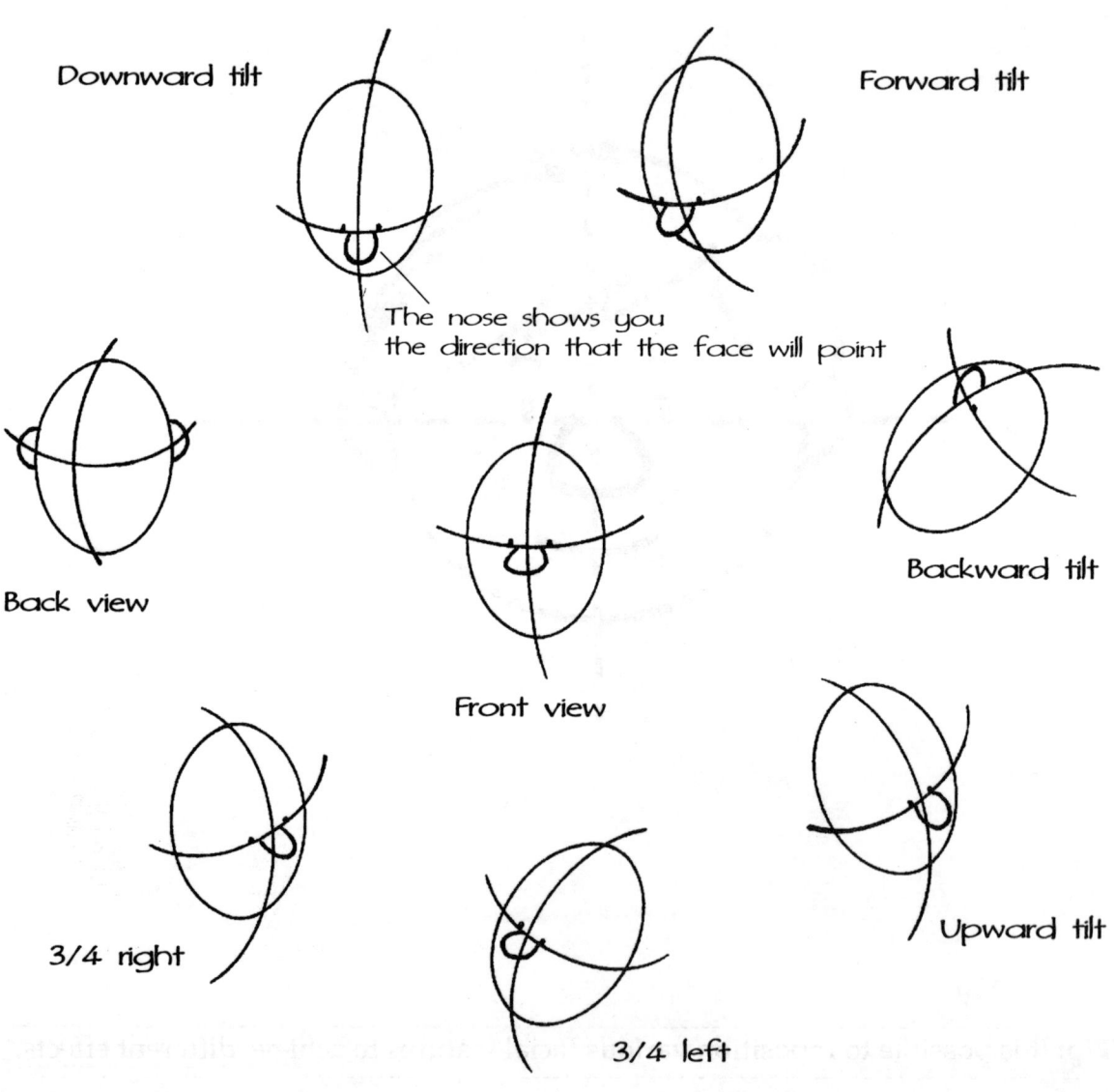

Downward tilt

Forward tilt

The nose shows you the direction that the face will point

Back view

Front view

Backward tilt

3/4 right

3/4 left

Upward tilt

FACIAL FEATURES

Eyes

Since eyes are the most expressive features on a face, they play a huge role in conveying a character's feelings and emotions.

Changing the shape of the eyes and tilting them in the right direction can add humour to the expression. Here are some typical cartoon eye expressions to create interesting comic characters.

Eye Direction

By tilting the eyes in the opposite direction, you strengthen the expression of a character looking left or right.

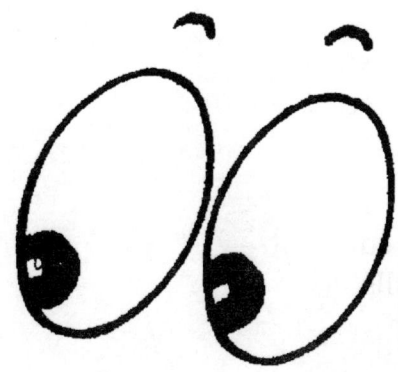

Eyes looking left, tilted right

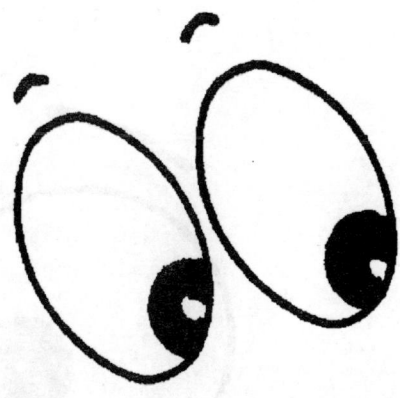

Eyes looking right, tilted left

Dotted
Simplest to draw for standard
cartoon expressions

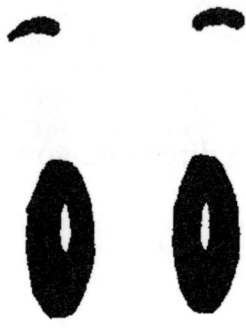

Round
Classic circular eyes pressed
together with small eyeballs.

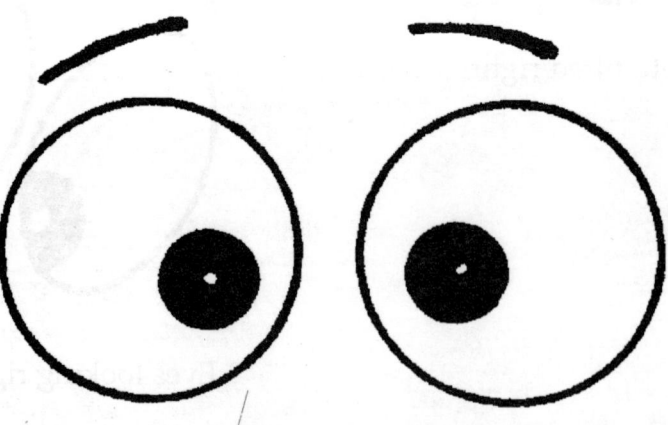

Overlapping
Stretched eyes pushed under one another for crazy expressions.

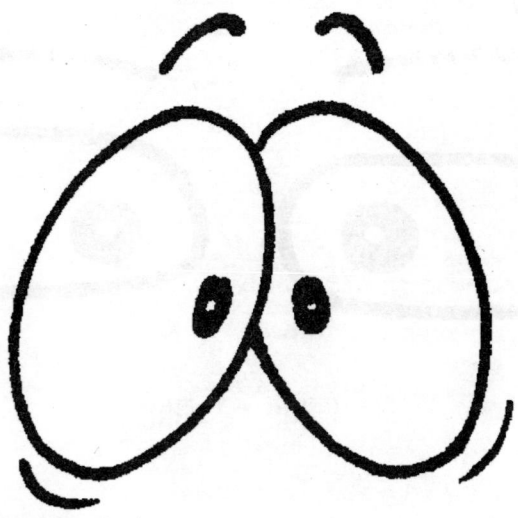

Droopy
Heavy eyelids and sloping eyes are drawn for tired and overworked characters.

Rectangular

Drawn for weird characters or a vacant stare;
Eyes spaced apart with small floating pupils.

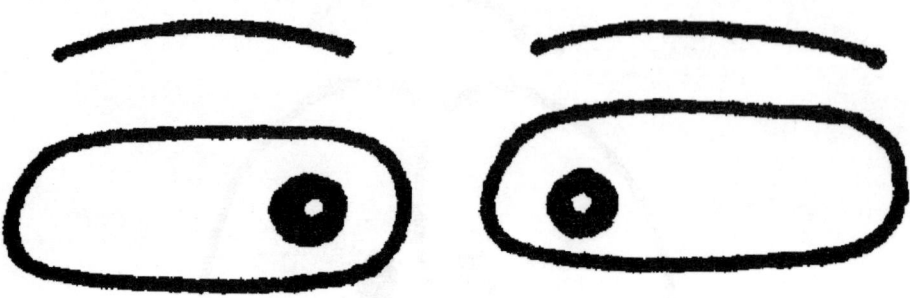

Intense

Heavy eyebrows crushing down the eyelids for mean characters.

Tip: The placement of eyebrows is very important. They should be lifted up and not too close to the eyes.

Nose

The central focus of the face is the cartoon nose. This influences the character and its personality and is meant to be funny.

Sharp

Beak

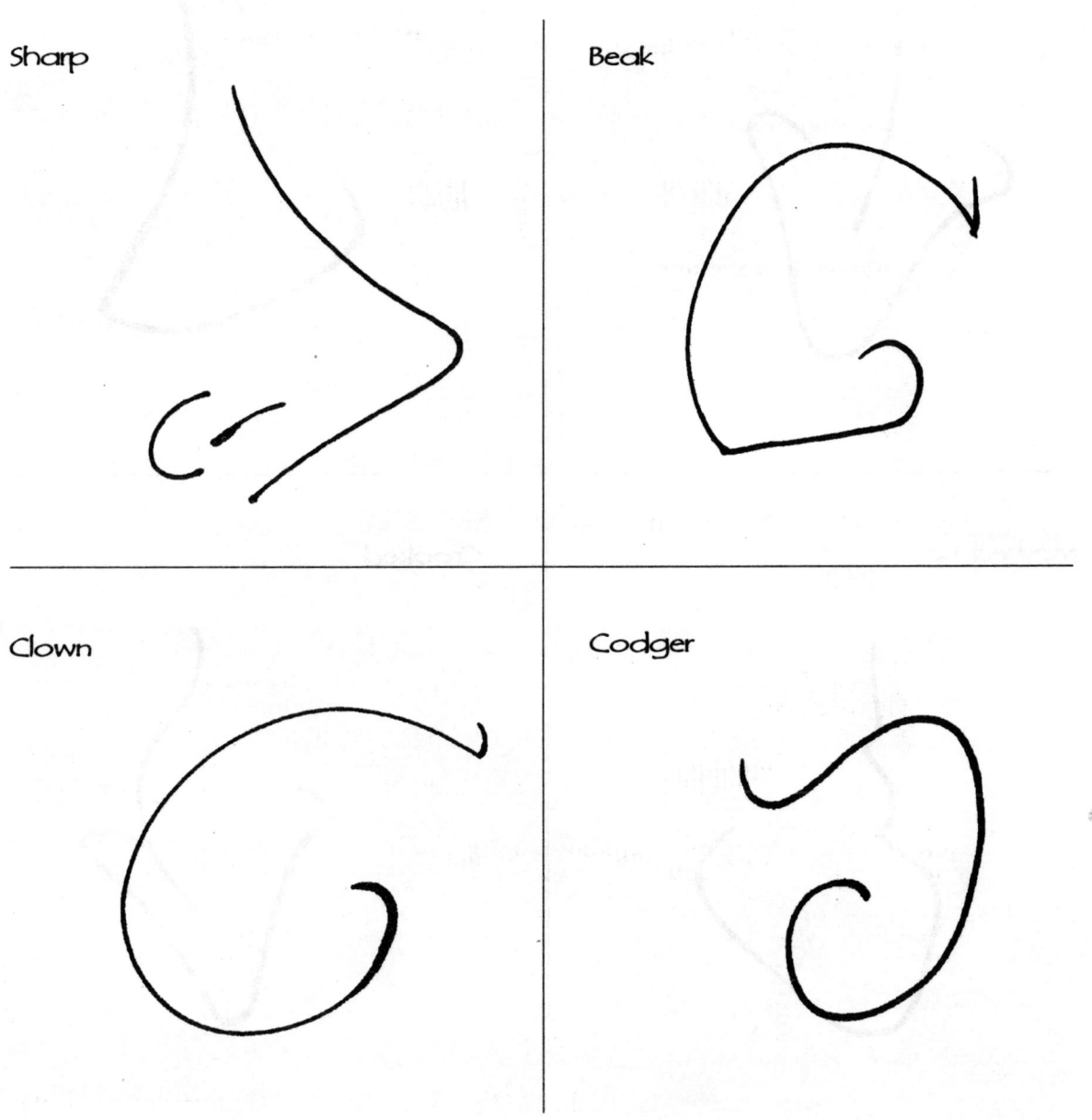

Clown

Codger

Pointed

Flat

Mashed up

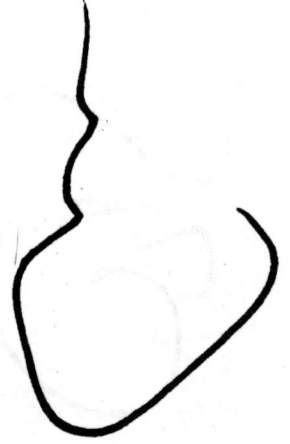

Crooked

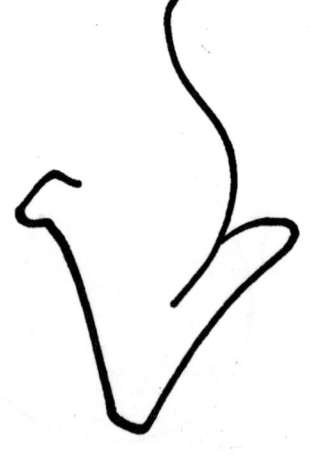

Triangular

Clover

Tiny

Droopy

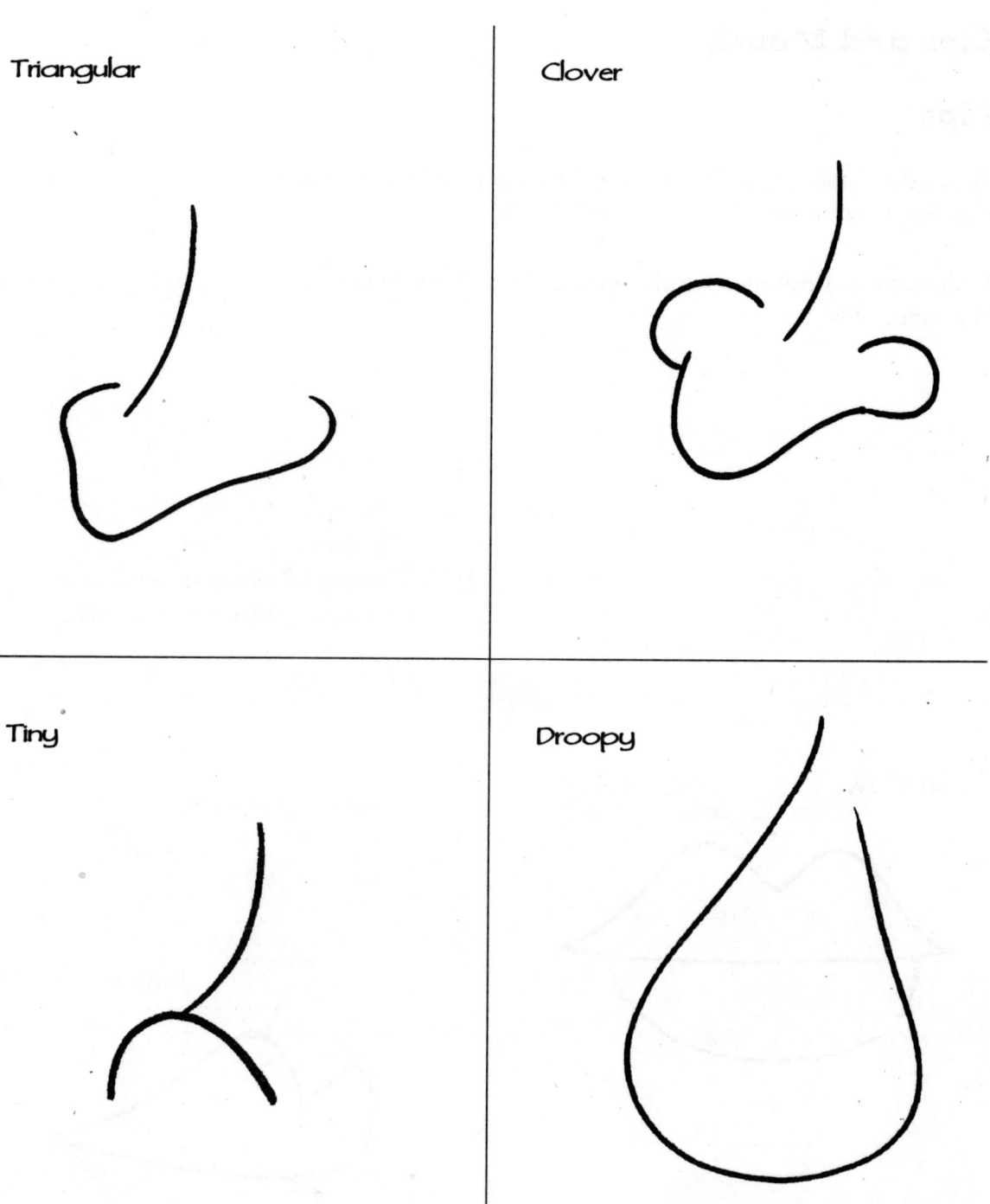

Tip: Drawing nostrils is optional.

Lips and Mouth

Lips

A single slash or a curved cupid's bow helps in expressing emotions. Lead characters or heroes are drawn with full lips.

Follow these references and you will learn how to decide on the lip type for your character.

Classic:
The cupid's bow is used to make a character more voluptuous.

Front View

Cupid's Bow

Side View

Simple lips

With no cupid's bow, these are the simplest to draw and used for funny characters.

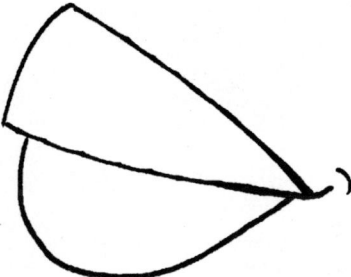

Common

Bow shaped with bigger upper lip, used to make the character more attractive.

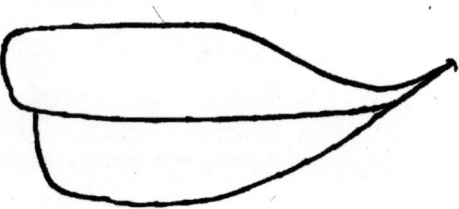

Pouty

Evenly drawn upper and bottom lips for pouty cartoon characters.

Big lower lip

Commonly used for creating unique characters.

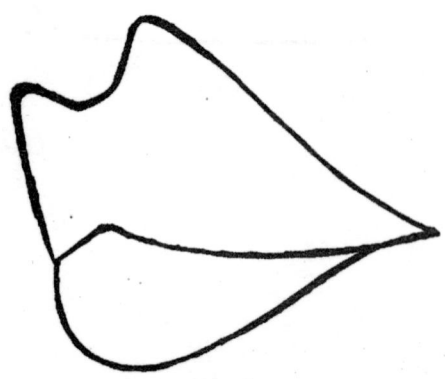

Mouth

The mouth conveys emotions best. Here are some mouth types you commonly see in cartoons.

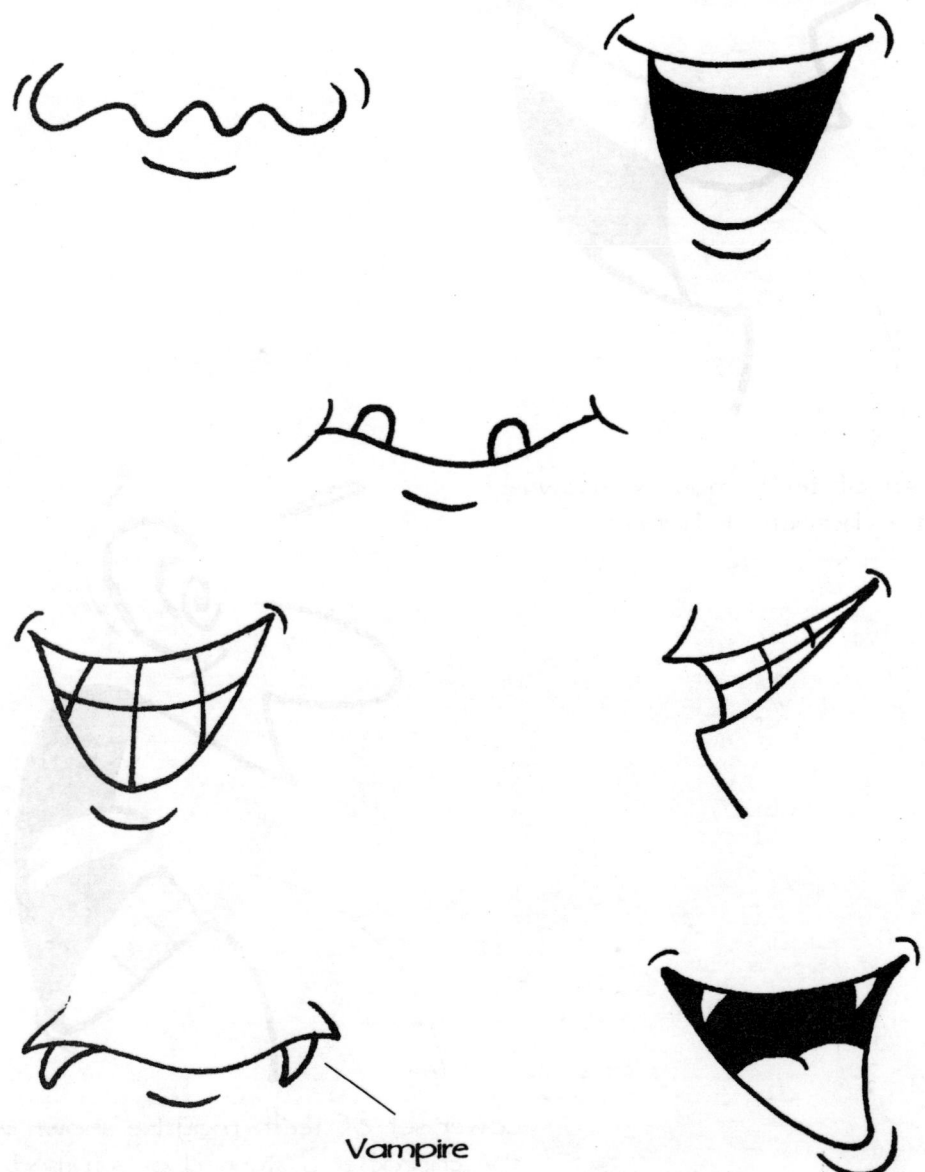

Vampire

Upper set of teeth may be shown when the character is happy.

Lower set of teeth may be shown when the character is stunned or surprised

Open mouth

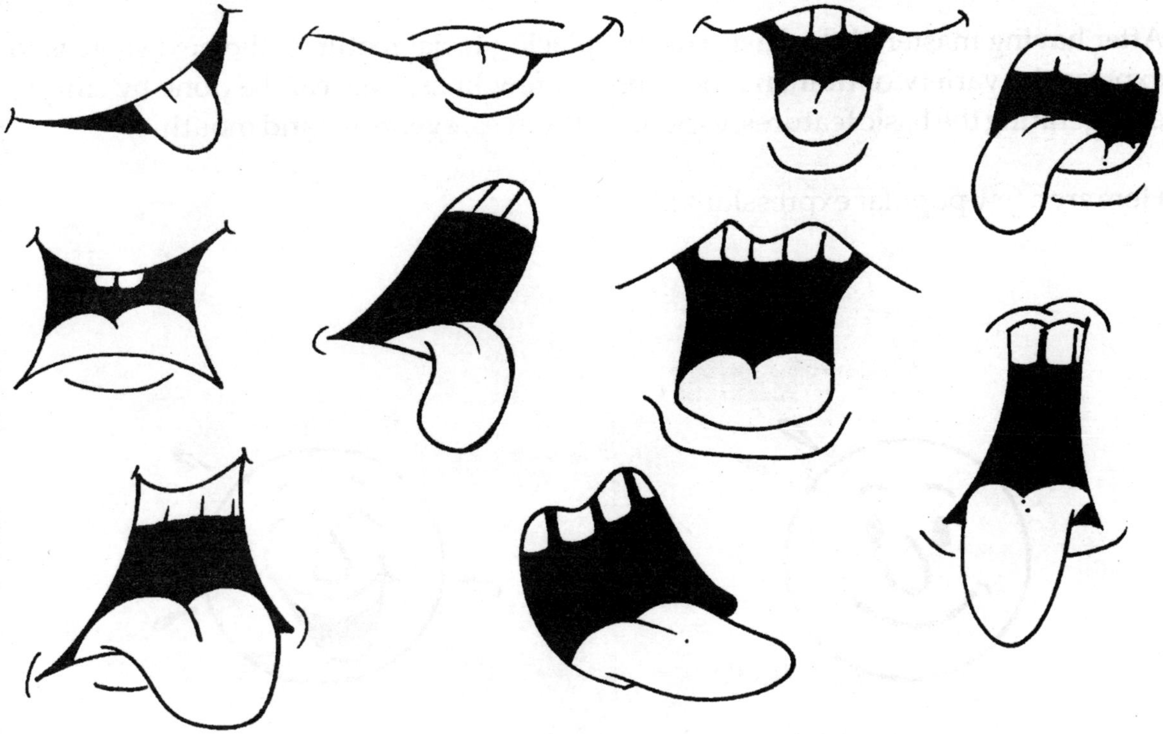

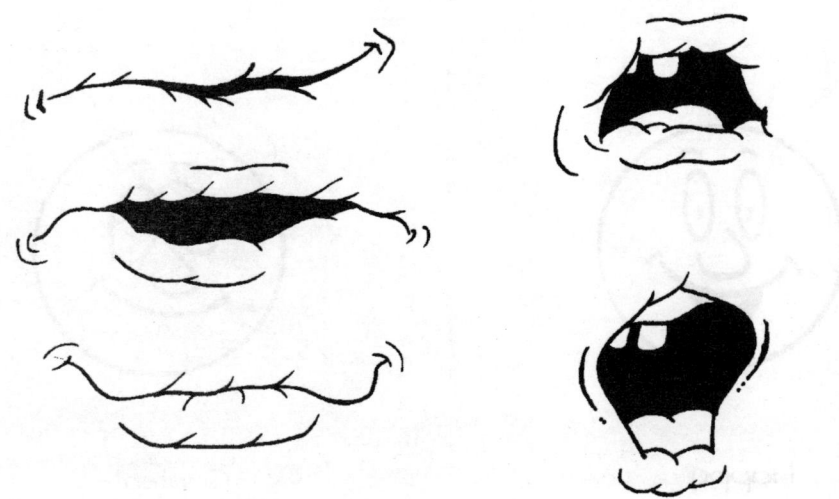

Oldies

EXPRESSIVE FACES

After having mastered the basic rule for placing facial features, the next stage is to express the variety of human emotions in a few lines. This can be done by simply exaggerating the basic features, especially the eyes, eyebrows and mouth.

Here are a few popular expressions:

Smiling

Laughing

Happy

Content

Annoyed

Upset

Angry

Furious

Evil

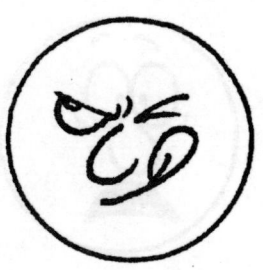

Scheming

Confused

Dumbstruck

Embarrassed

Afraid

Frightened

Shocked

Suspicious

Sneering

Hurt

Shouting

Weary

Worried

Optimistic

Confident

Drunk

Knocked out

Surprised

Thoughtful

Painful

Crying

Yawning

Sad

Tip: Most of the action occurs in the eyes and the mouth.

Extreme Expressions

Once you have mastered the basic expressions, you will want to move into more advanced and zany expressions. Modern age cartoons exhibit wild and over-the-top expressions called **takes**. Follow these examples:

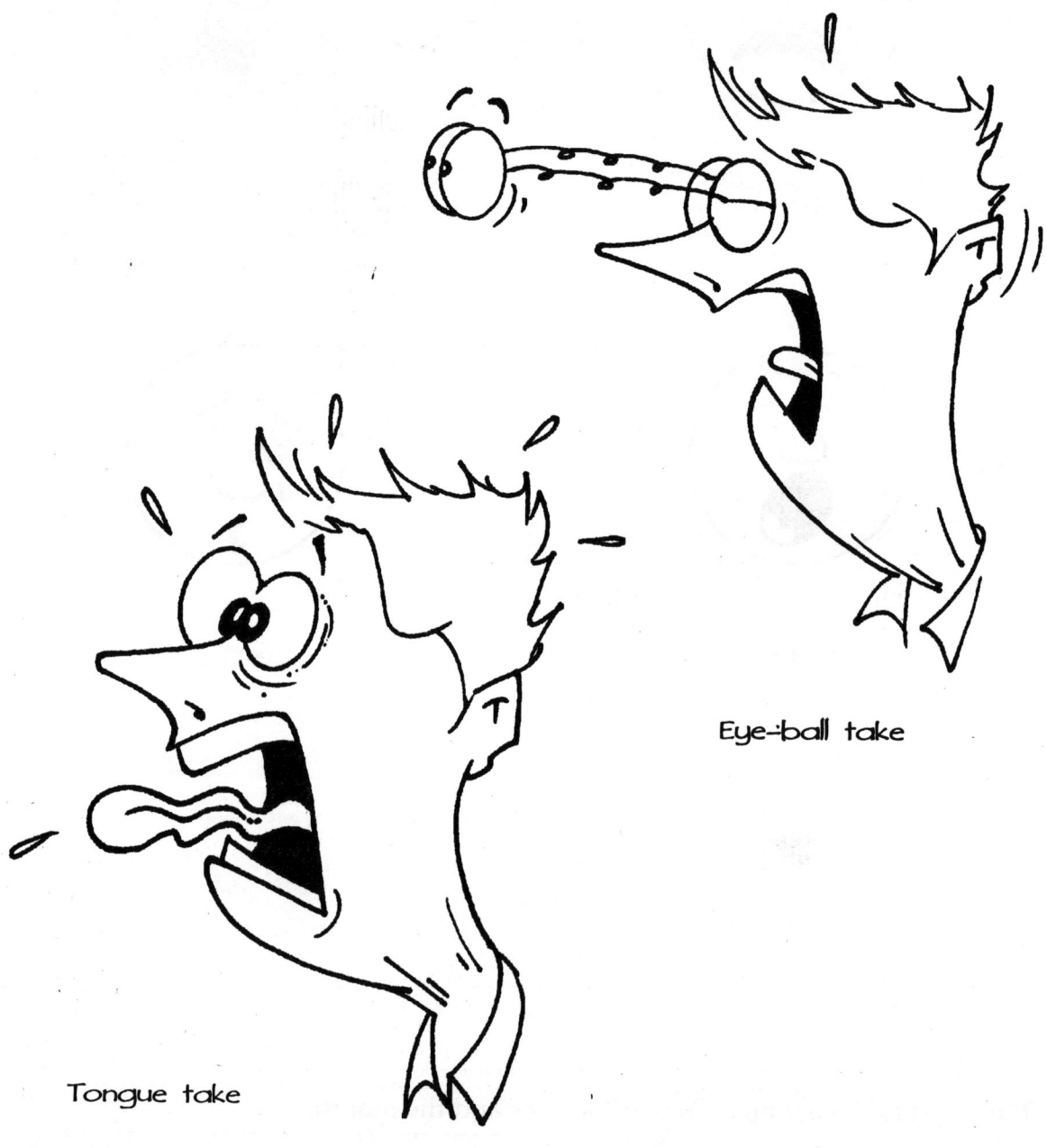

Eye-ball take

Tongue take

Jaw-drop take

Hair take

CHEEKS AND CHIN

Add a goofy look to any character by changing the shapes of the cheeks and chin.

Make the chins protrude to set them apart from real people.

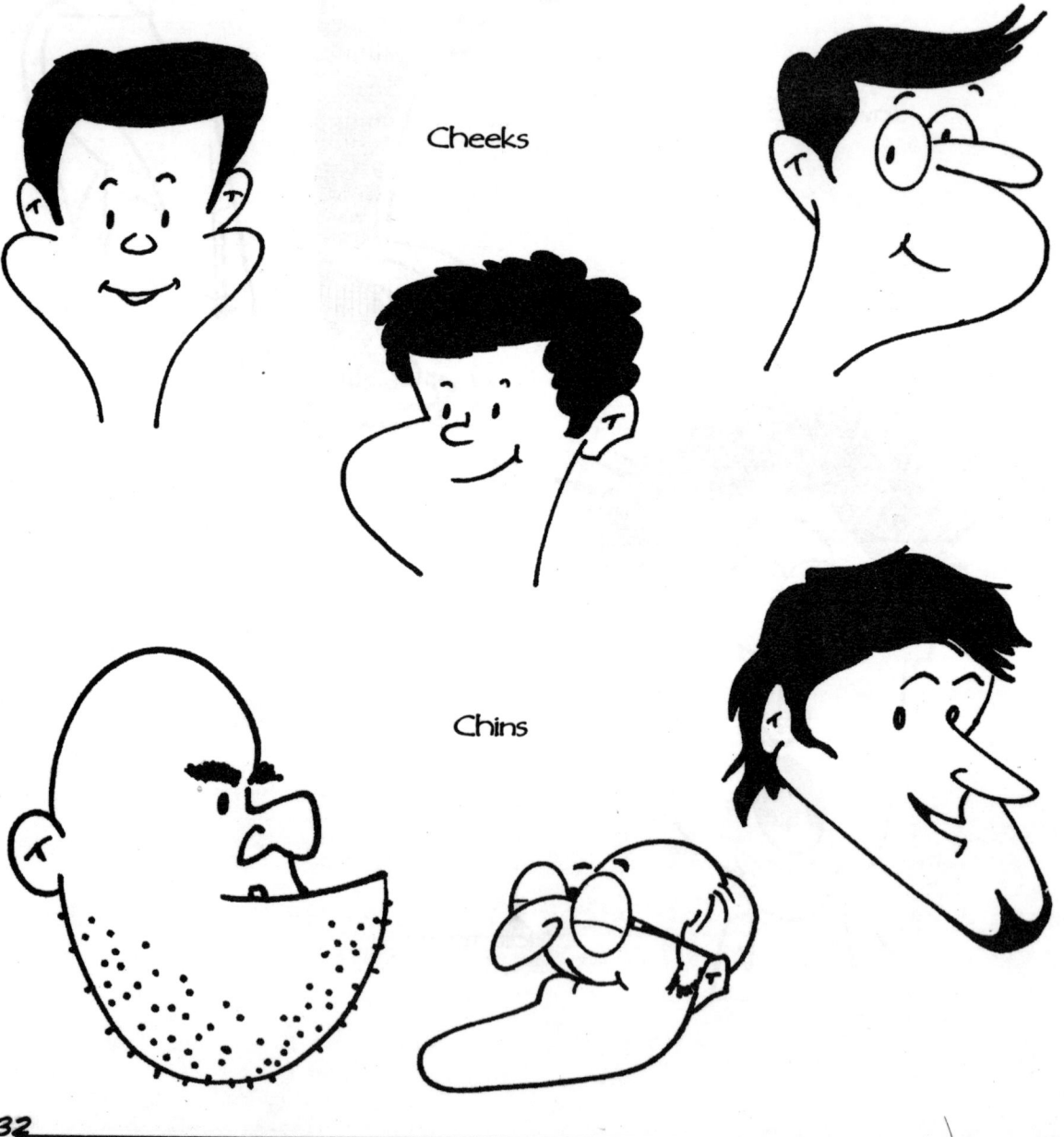

Cheeks

Chins

NECK AND SHOULDERS

Both combined together create one cartoon character . You can match the body type to the neck to make your cartoon characters interesting.

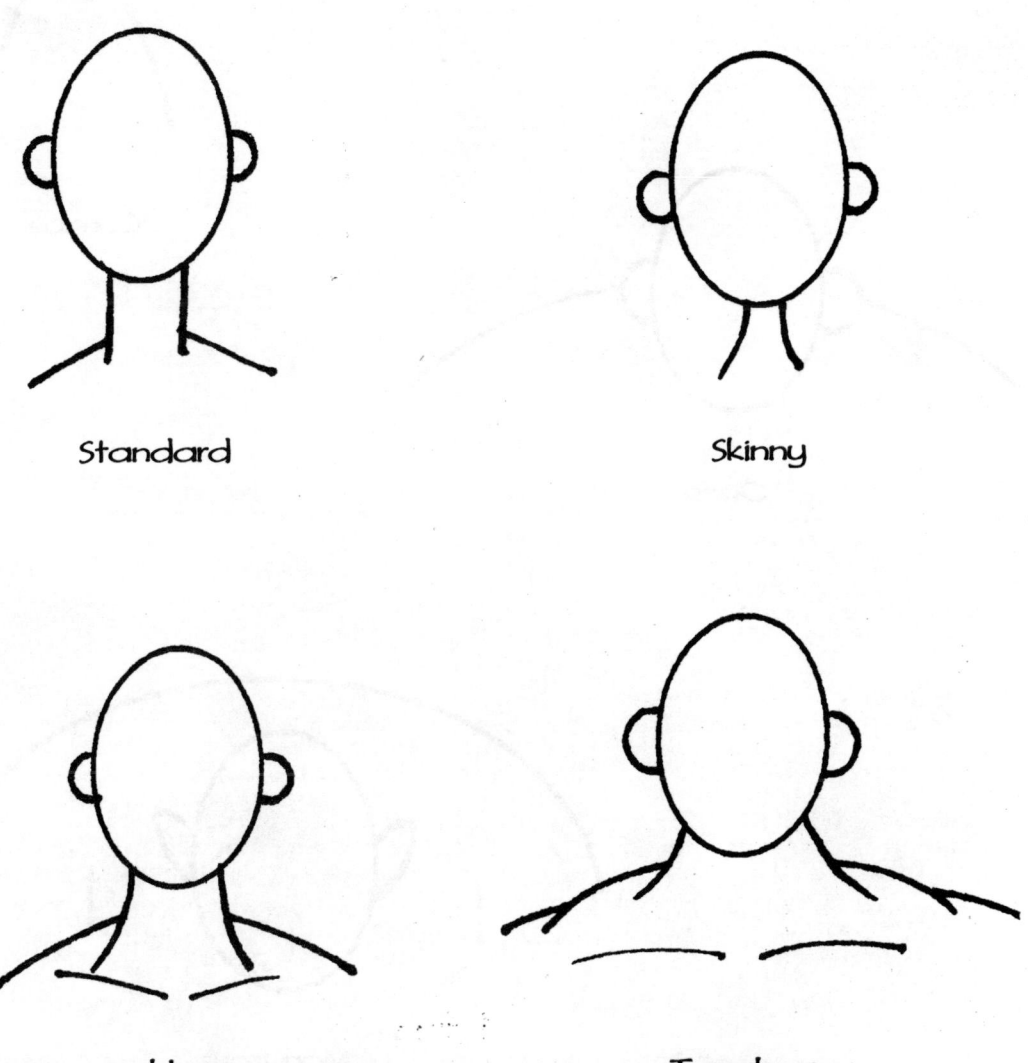

Standard

Skinny

Hero

Tough guy

Neckless types

Comical

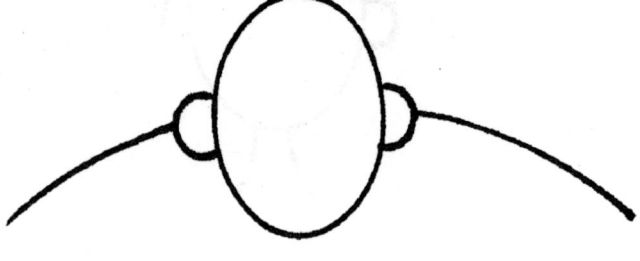

Obese

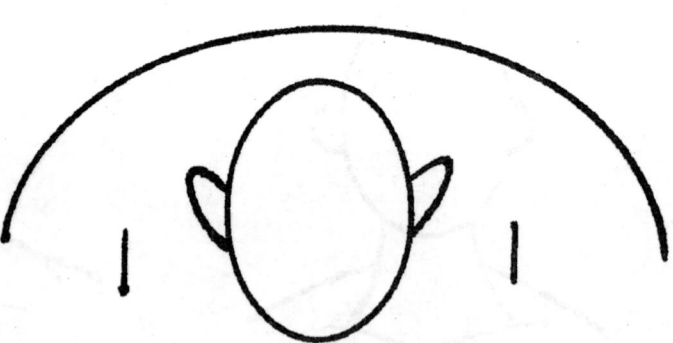

Monstrous

Shoulders

Whether the shoulders slump or are held squarely has a huge effect on the character's posture or personality.

Male basics

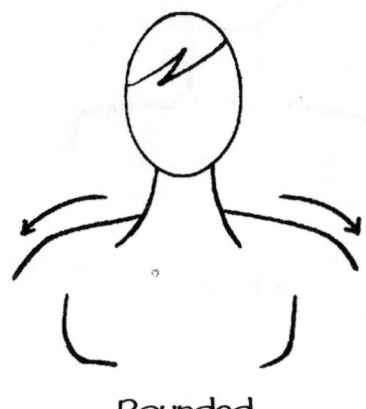

Rounded

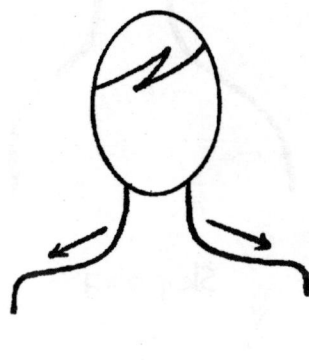

Flat

Looks unnatural and tense

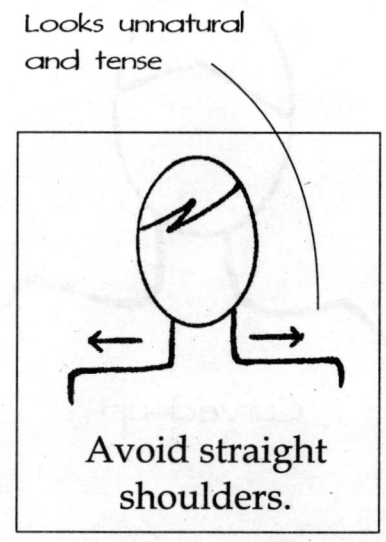

Avoid straight shoulders.

Female

Sloping

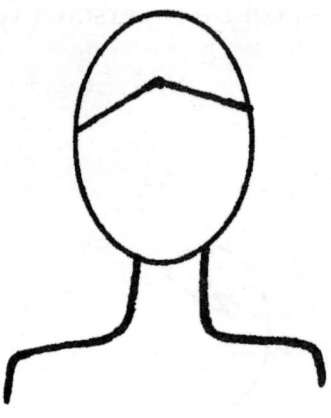

Square

Curved-up

MATCHSTICK FIGURES

An action line is the foundation of a good pose, especially when the body is shown bending, twisting, turning or moving. Stick figures make it easy to show different actions.

Cartoon Walk

You can give a your character a unique personality through his or her walk.

Standard

Peppy

Cool

Forceful

Perspective in cartoon walk

The front foot is larger than the backfoot.

The action line follows the natural curve of the spine. It is the foundation that conveys the direction of a pose.

Cartoon Run

Whether a character is being chased or is chasing something or someone, the posture should match the pace of the action.

Standard

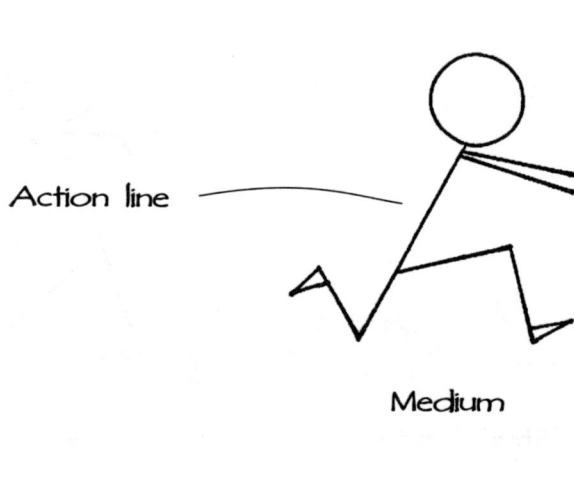

Action line

Medium

Extreme

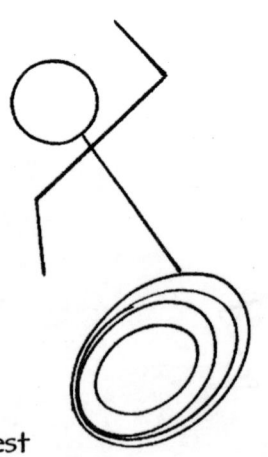

Fastest

Pose using Arc

To make a smooth flowing motion, the action should follow an arc.

Arc

Tip: Not all action lines are action-oriented, some simply bind the body together from head to toe.

Matching the body's attitude with the
facial expression is important.

Angry

Sneaky

Crying

Wicked

Funny

Knocked-out

CLOTHING AND FOLDS

It is not the design of the clothing but the loops, folds and creases caused when the person moves that need to be convincingly drawn.

Sleeve folds

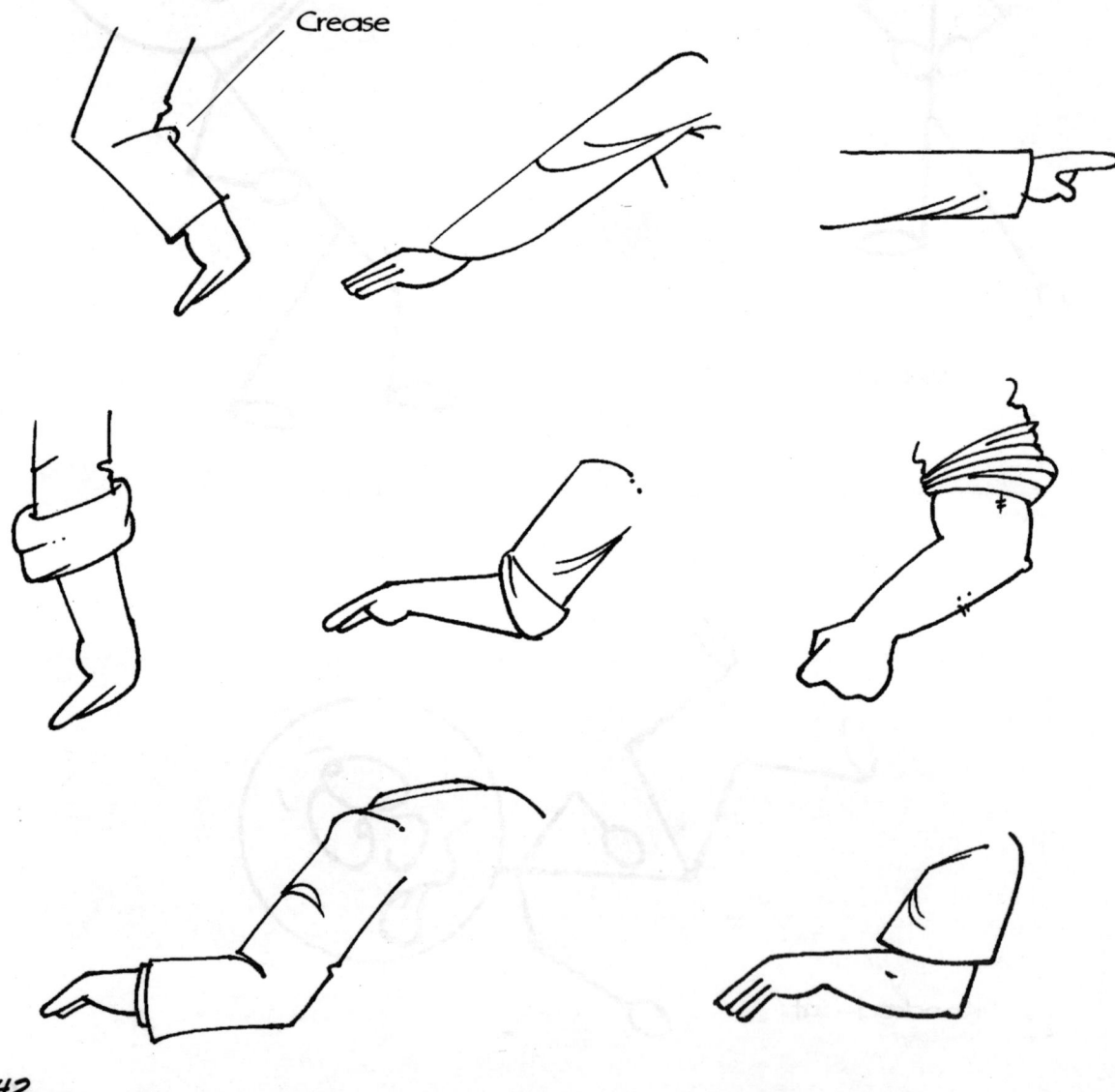

Crease

Long and Short Creases

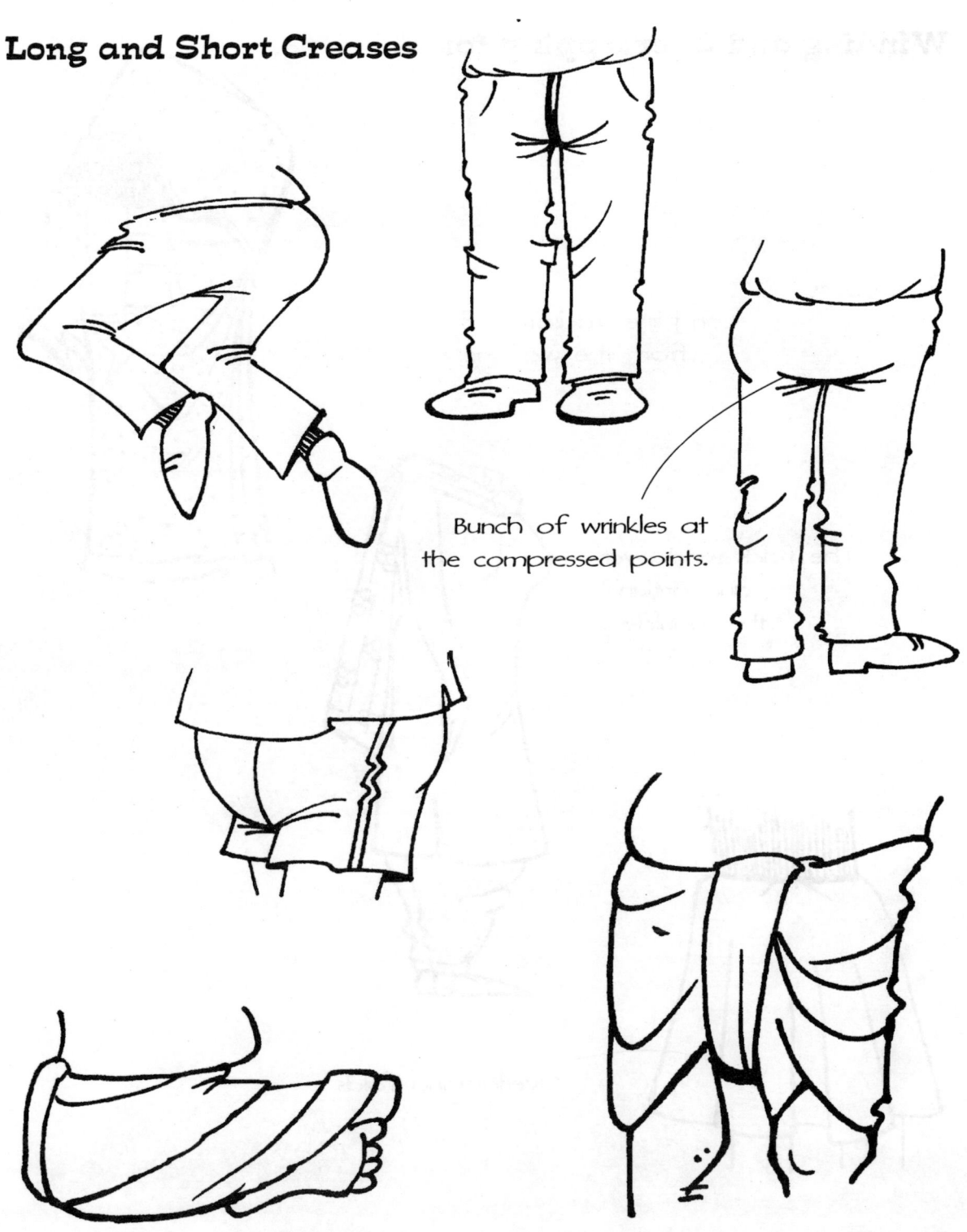

Bunch of wrinkles at the compressed points.

Winding and Overlapping folds

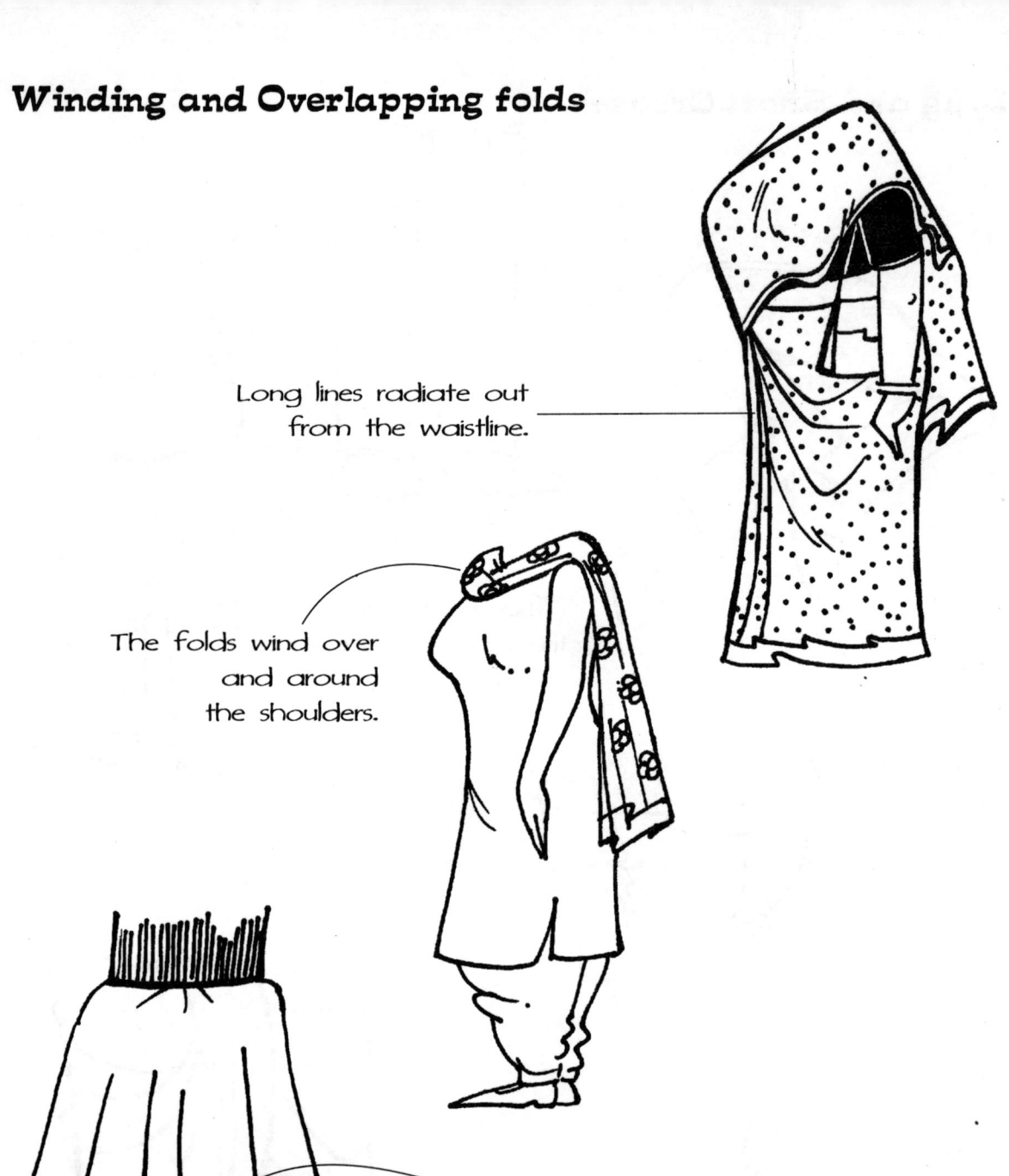

Long lines radiate out from the waistline.

The folds wind over and around the shoulders.

Overlapping folds

HANDS

For a cartoonist, the hand is invaluable as an expressive part of the cartoon character. For example, a clenched fist indicates anger, hands, and a finger pressed to the lips means silence.

In the cartoon world, hand poses range from realistic to the animator's three-finger technique, which is now a standard practice.

As long as the hand is drawn convincingly, the number of fingers is not important. But keep it consistent for every character.

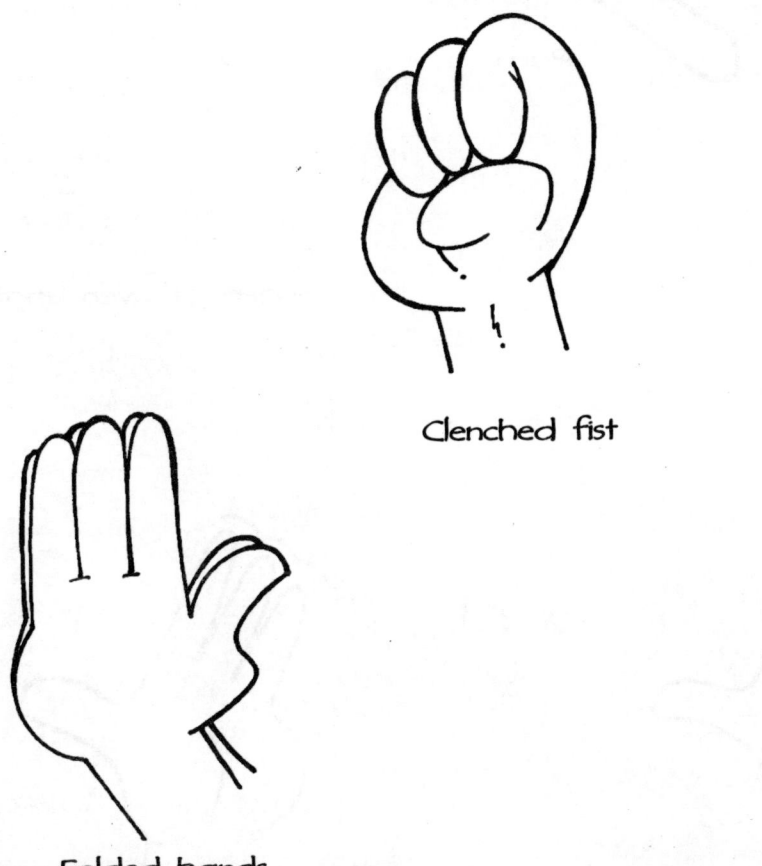

Clenched fist

Folded hands

Pointed finger

Classic cartoon hand

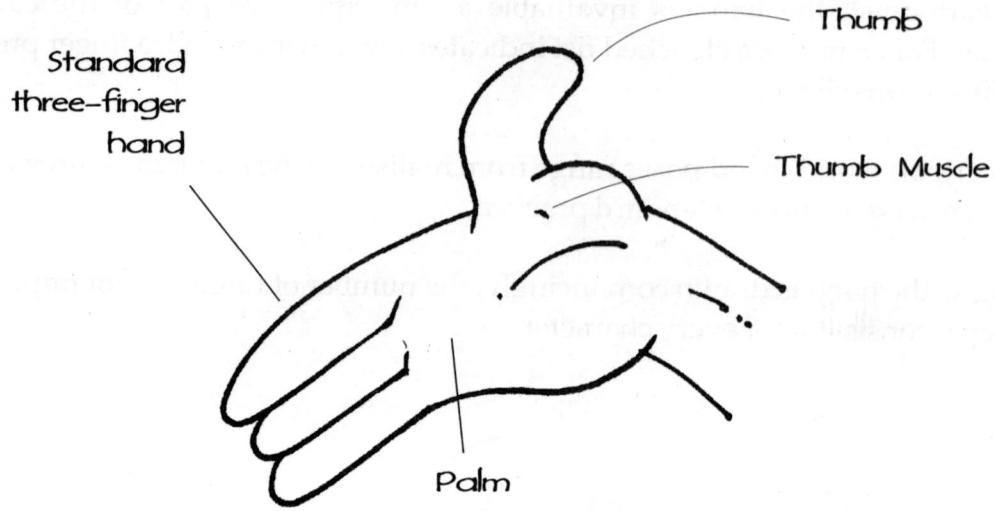

Thumb

Thumb Muscle

Standard
three-finger
hand

Palm

Uneven fingers which
diminish in size

Fingers of even length

Hand types

Steel fists, feeble fingers, plump palms, gnarled knuckles–each hand has a unique personality depending upon the aspect you want to emphasise.

Female
Tapered and thin fingers with painted fingertips

Kid
Short and chubby

Senior Citizen
Skinny and large with curled fingers and protruding bones.

Teen/Adult
Regular hand, not too bony.

Variations in pointing gestures

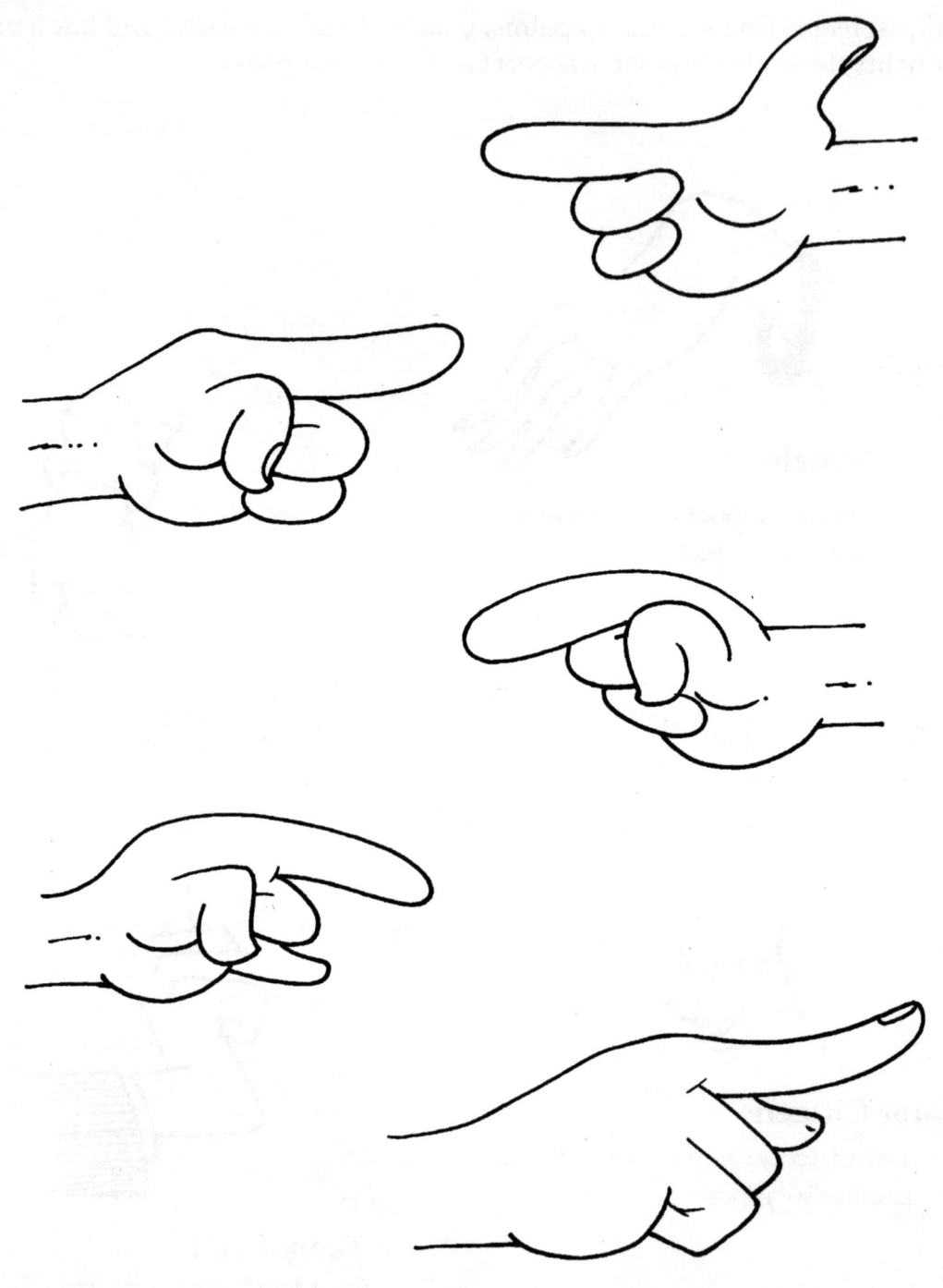

Hands in action

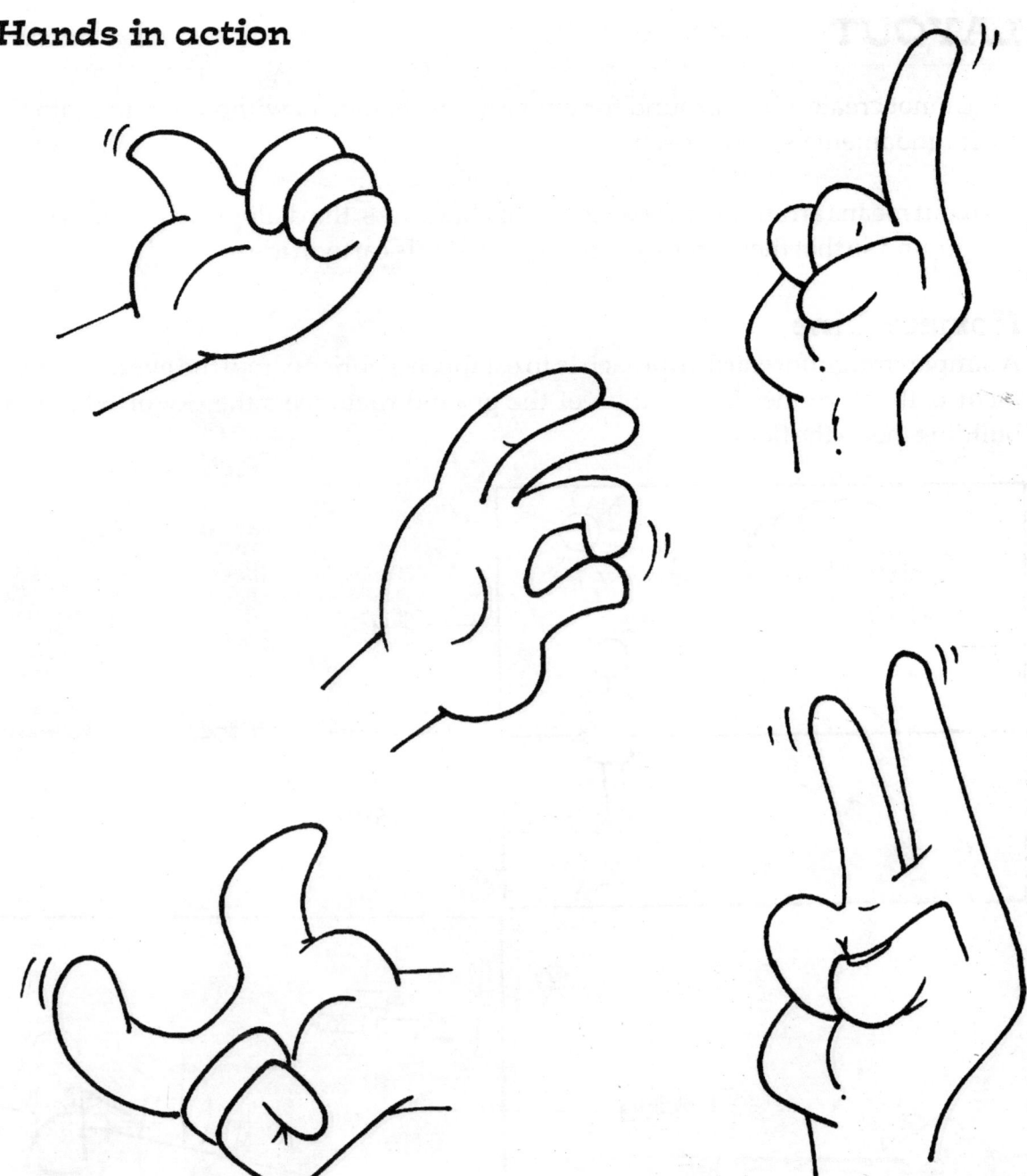

Tip: The gap between the fingers should not be too wide. Any pose can be made to look more realistic by allowing the fingers to cross or overlap.

LAYOUT

We cannot create a background for our cartoon characters without getting into the basic fundamentals of perspective.

A layout means arranging the background characters, the dialogue balloon, and the foreground so that they interact to promote a single cartoon idea.

Horizon Line

A simple straightforward approach is to establish a horizon line–the eye level of the picture. It determines the location of the ground that meets the sky or where the building meets the floor.

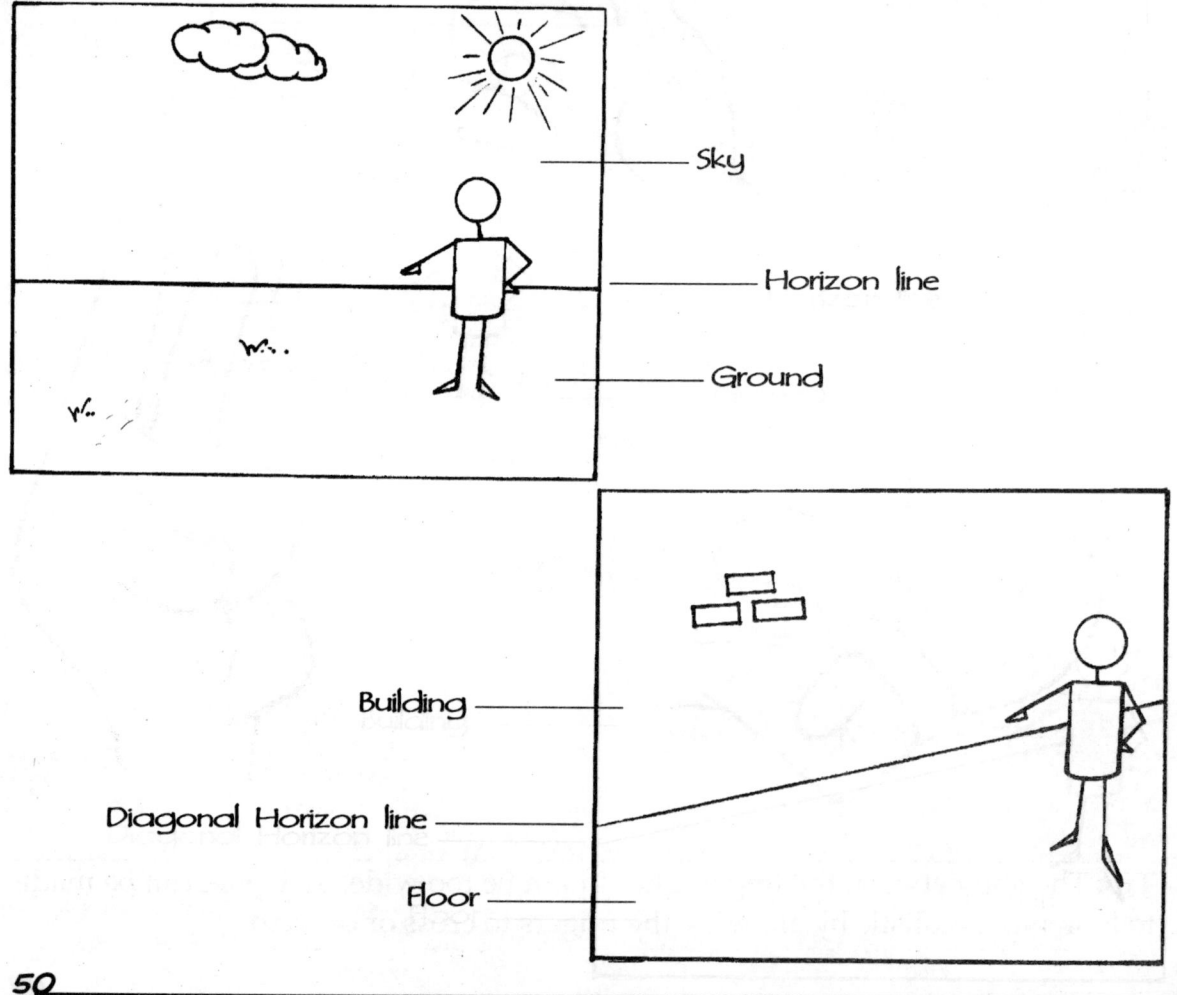

Varying heights of the horizon line

Remember, wherever your character stands in the picture, the horizon line will always cross them just below the knees.

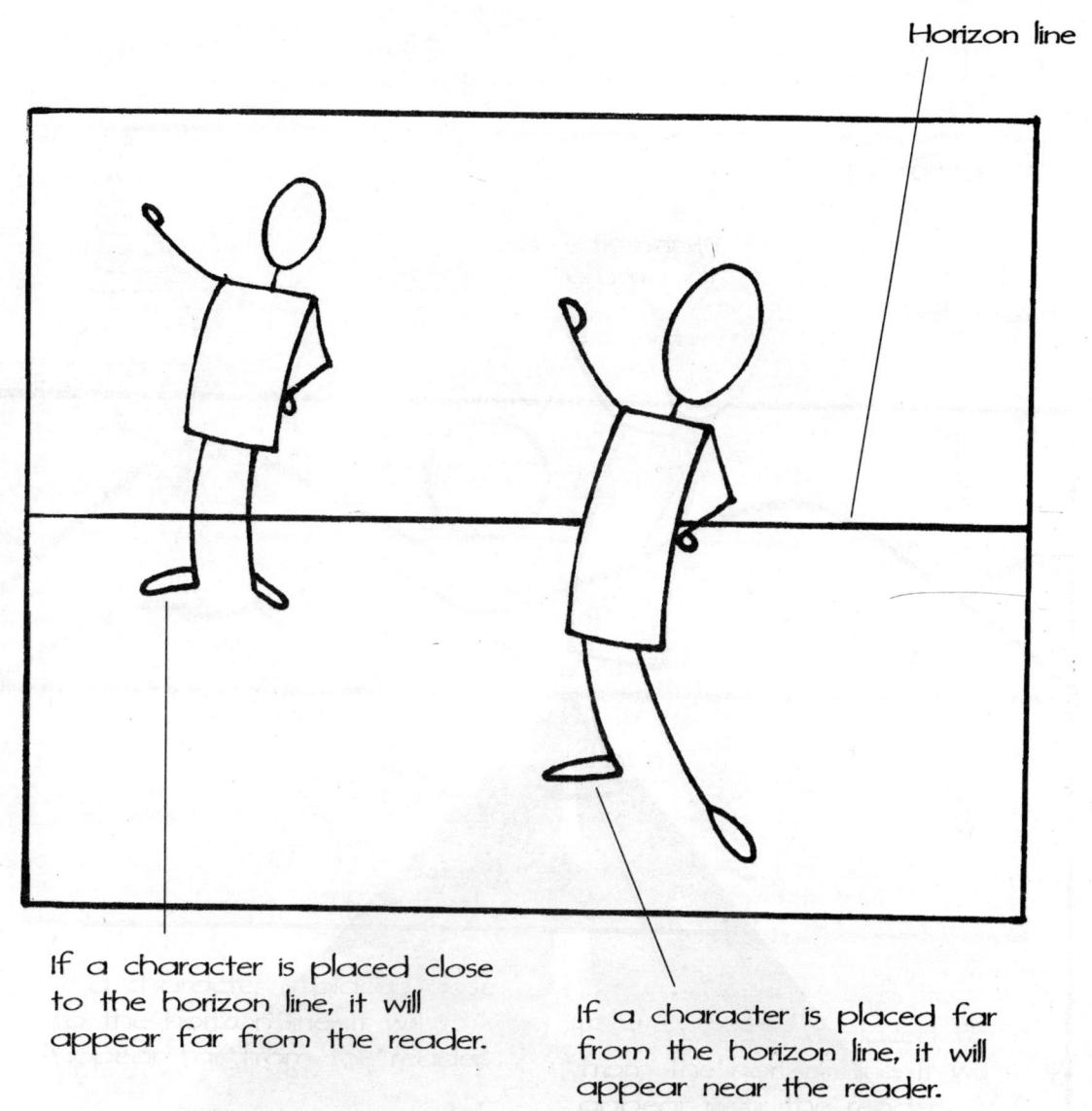

Horizon line

If a character is placed close to the horizon line, it will appear far from the reader.

If a character is placed far from the horizon line, it will appear near the reader.

Tip: The horizon line can be effectively used to position your background and character in the right proportion.

Vanishing point

It is the point where two parallel lines appear to meet or vanish towards the horizon line. It creates an illusion of depth or distance, for example, a standard cartoon railway track or road.

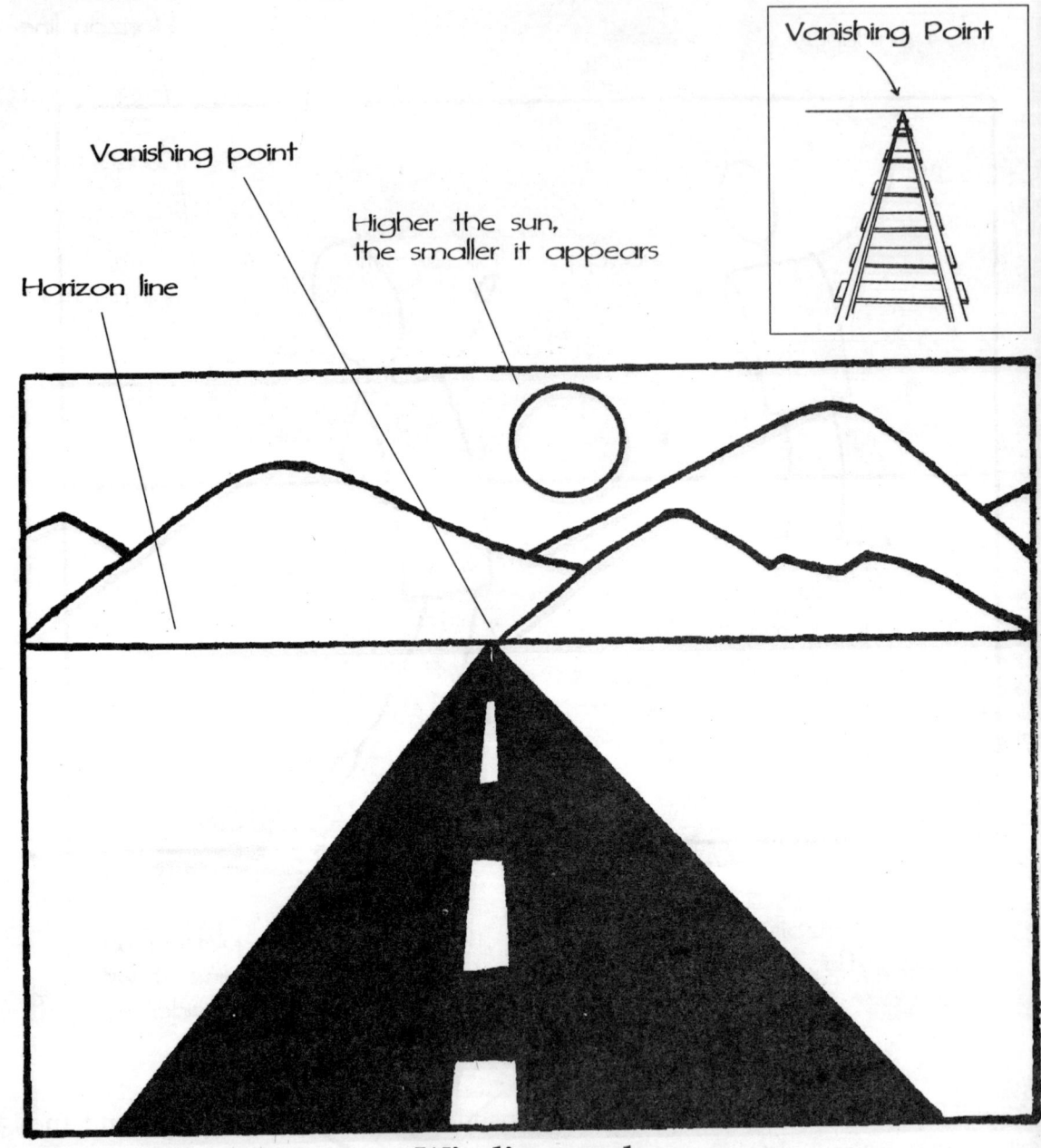

Vanishing Point

Vanishing point

Horizon line

Higher the sun, the smaller it appears

Winding road

Lower the sun, the larger it appears

Highway

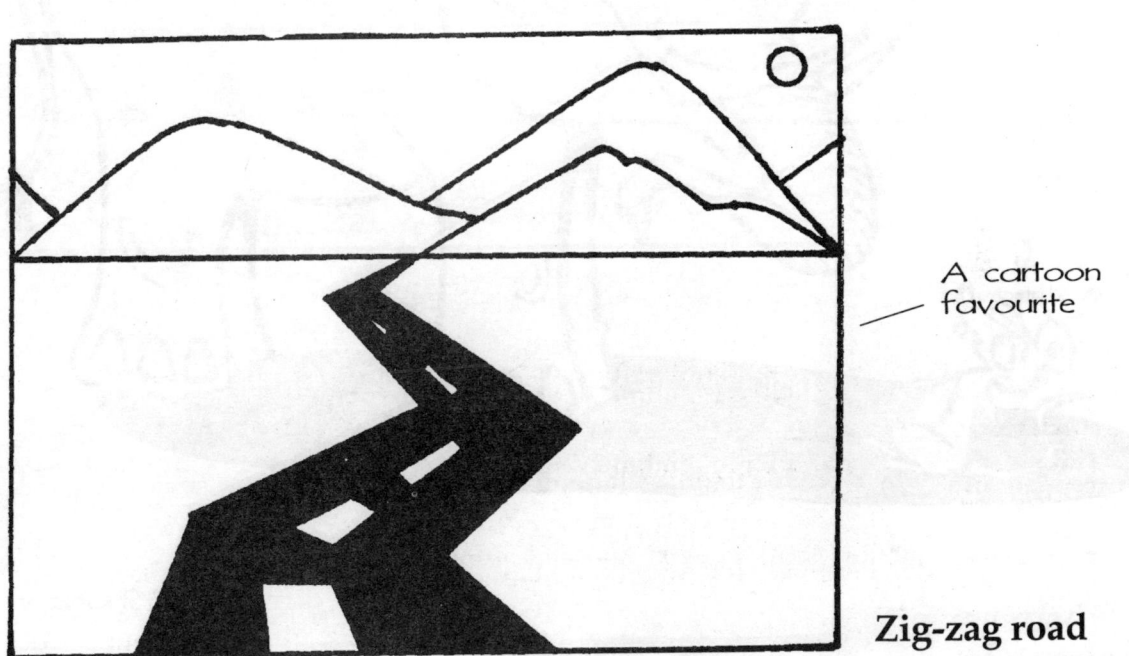

A cartoon favourite

Zig-zag road

Layout Tricks

Shadows

To show a character as bigger and stronger than another, cartoonists add shadows underneath the character to create a sense of weight.

Shadow

Hidden shapes

You will find a hidden shape in the space between two objects or characters drawn together.

This space looks like a heart

Simple room layout

To show depth, you can draw the corner of a room in two ways.

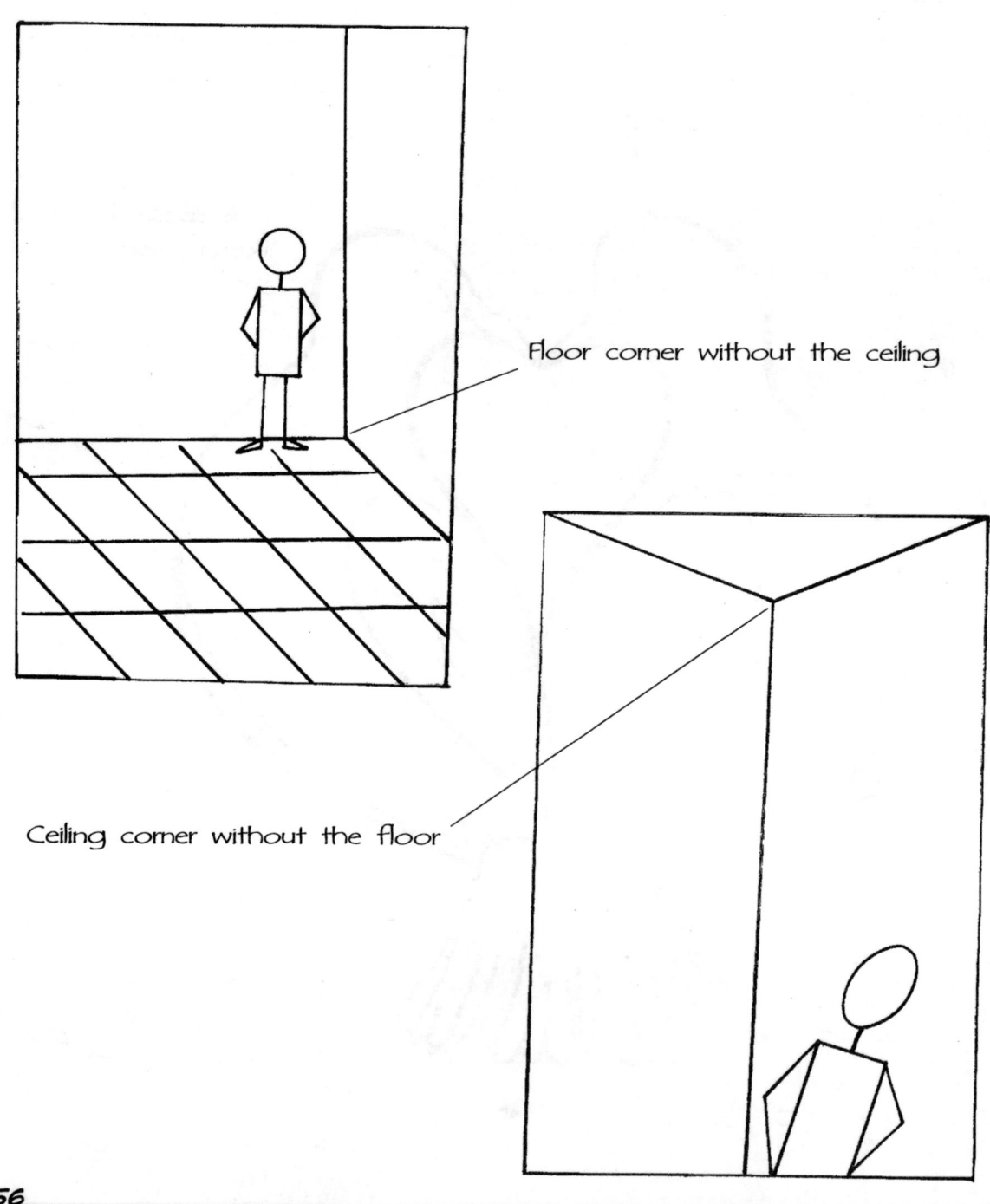

Floor corner without the ceiling

Ceiling corner without the floor

Corners

The surprise element in a cartoon can be enhanced using corners.

Tip: Avoid drawing the props and the backgrounds realistically. Exaggerate, interpret and keep everything cartoonish.

LETTERING EFFECTS

There are two types of lettering that emphasise delivery of speech. One is contained within a speech bubble or caption.

The other is the fancy lettering floating in the cartoon area and visually describing sound effects or human utterances.

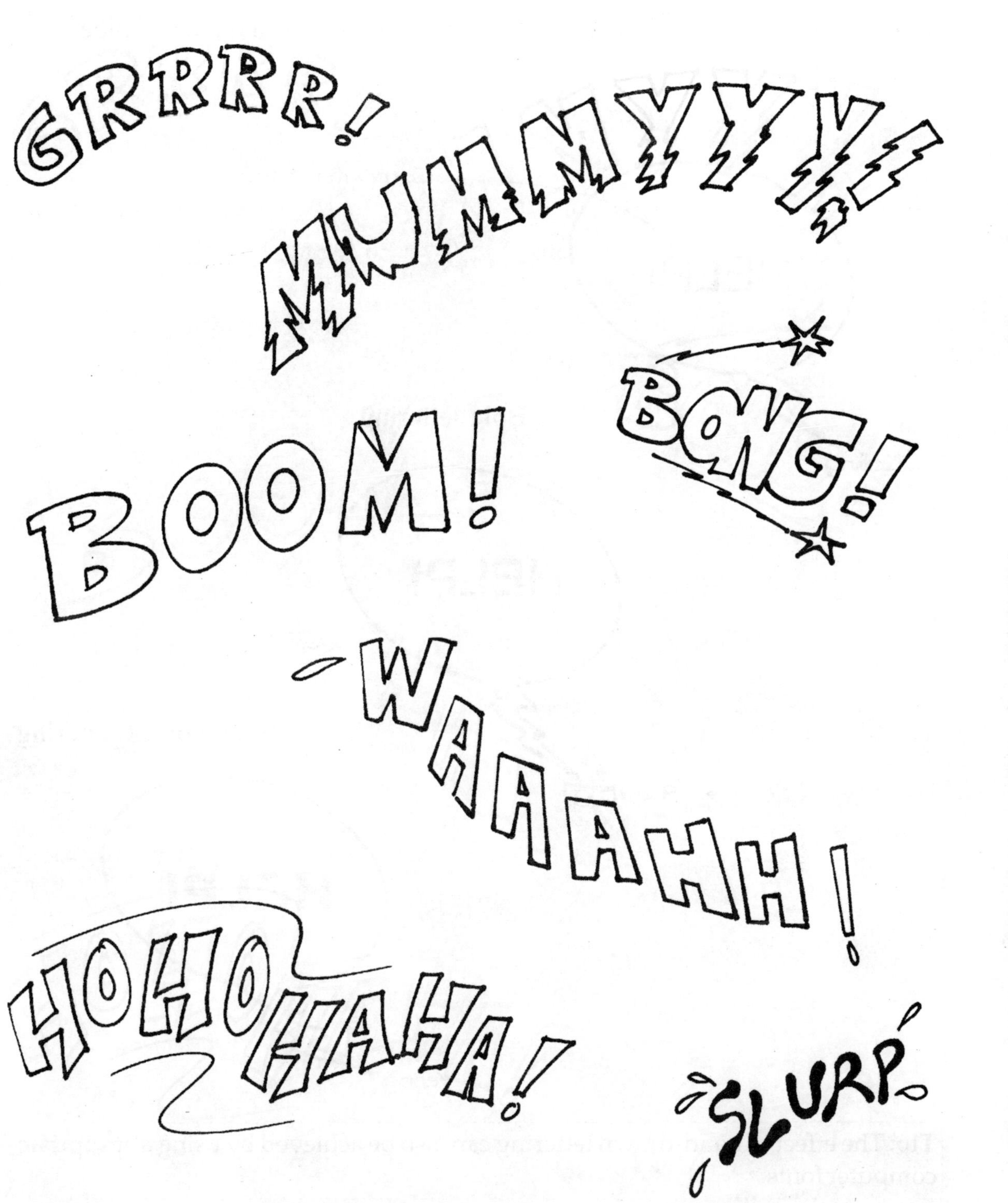
GRRRRR!
MUMMYYY!
BOOM!
BONG!
WAAAAHH!
HOHOHAHA!
SLURP

Here are some lettering styles to indicate the volume of a character's voice.

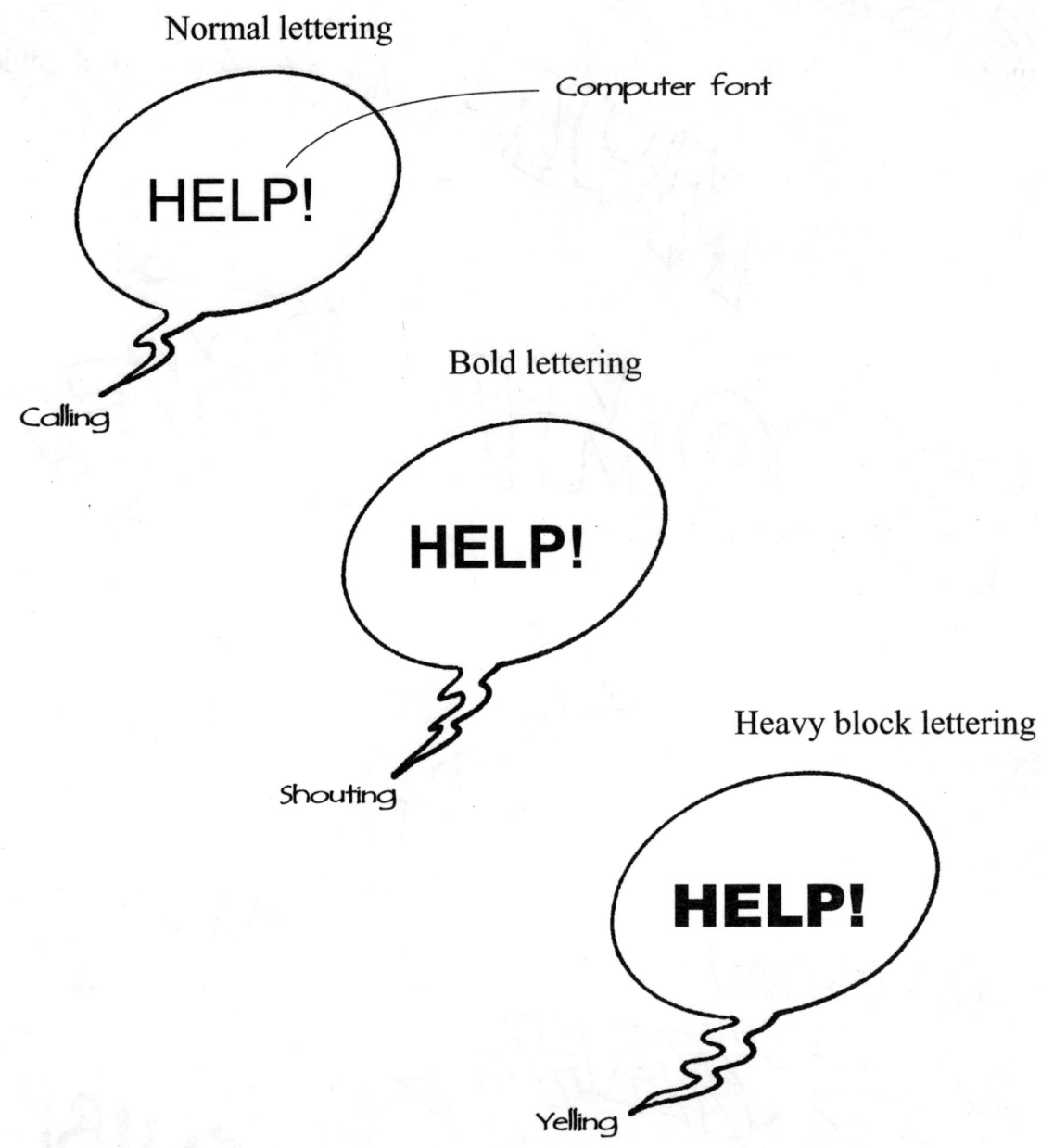

Normal lettering

Computer font

HELP!

Calling

Bold lettering

HELP!

Shouting

Heavy block lettering

HELP!

Yelling

Tip: The effect of hand-drawn lettering can also be achieved by using appropriate computer fonts.

SPEECH BUBBLES

Not all cartoons require words. If characters are speaking to one another, the message can be conveyed through speech, dialogue balloons and bubbles, which are white spaces with text enclosed within a border.

Below are some treatments that you could consider as your cartoon voices and thoughts. It won't take you long to decide which balloon works for you.

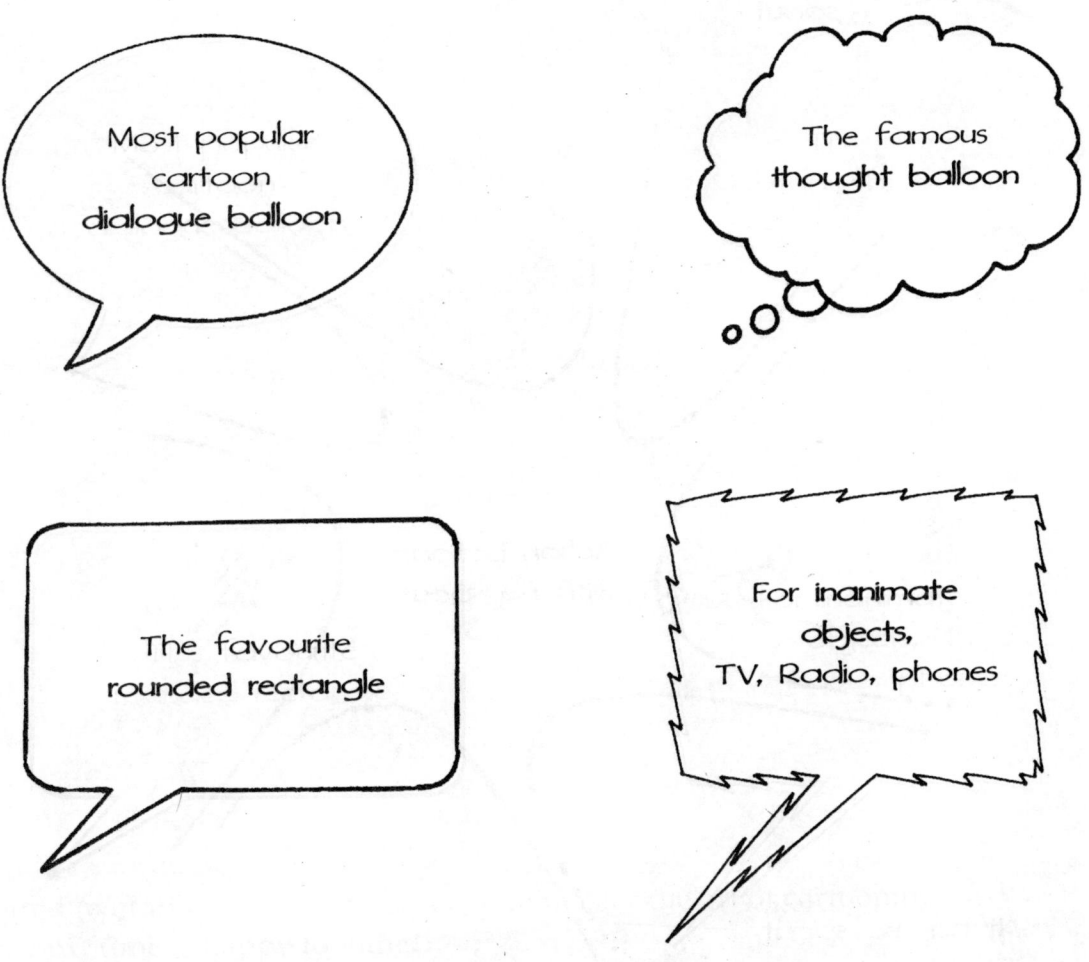

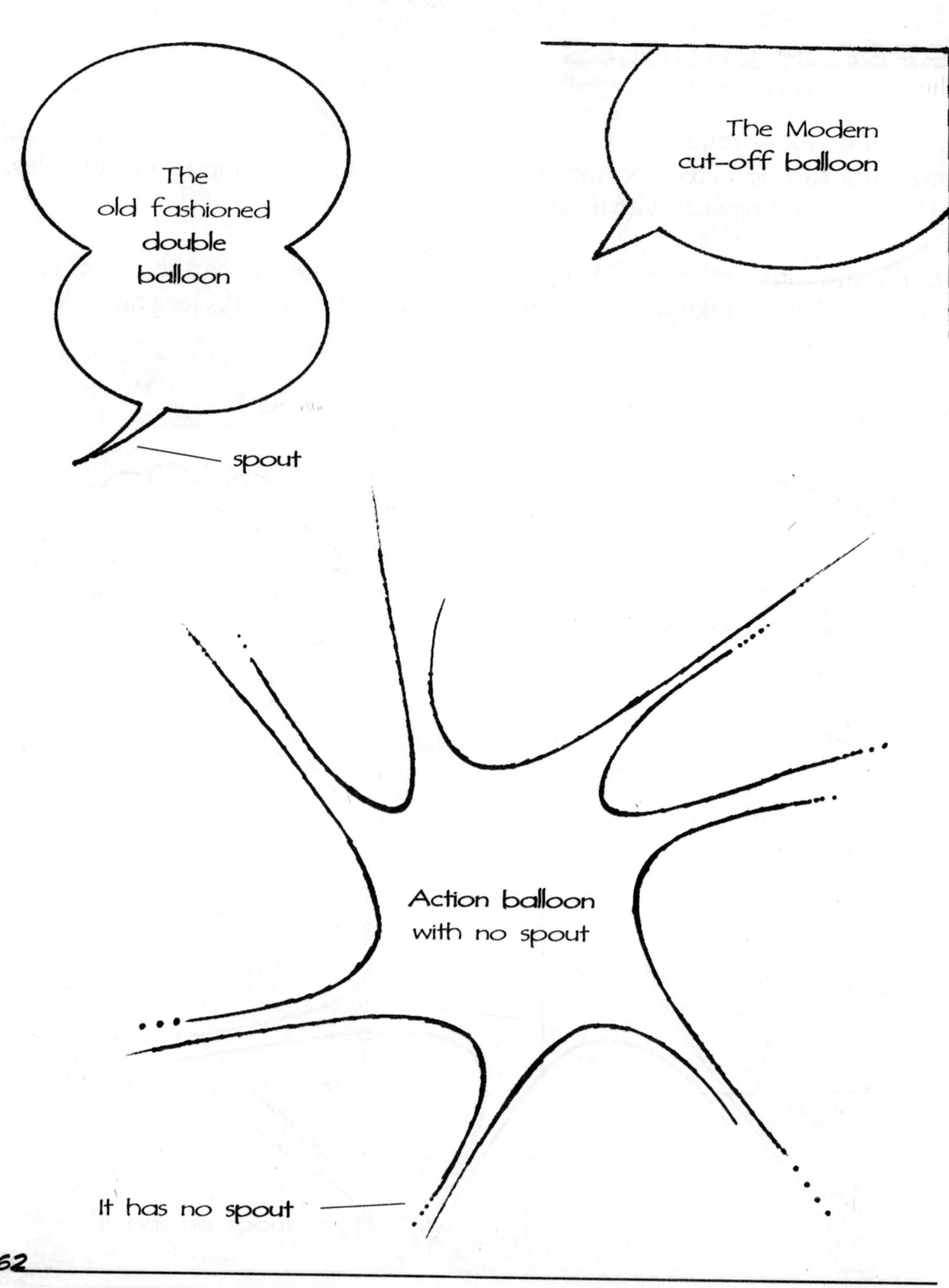

Rules for Speech Bubbles

The speech bubble of the character speaking first should be placed farthest to the left, and that of the character speaking next should be lower.

Cartoon animals speak to each other as well as with humans mostly through thought balloons.

Human babies interact with adults through thought balloons.

I have a weird feeling about this!

Longer spouts look weirder

Cutie – pie!

Wanna pee!

Where is your speech bubble?

I am sorry!

Borderless bubbles

Don't mix different styles of speech bubbles.

Tip: Make sure the spout of your speech balloon points to the character who is speaking.

COMIC GIMMICKS

Cartoonists employ various techniques to indicate movement, noise, action and mood that hint at what is happening or is about to happen without using words.

Here are a few examples to bring your cartoons to life.

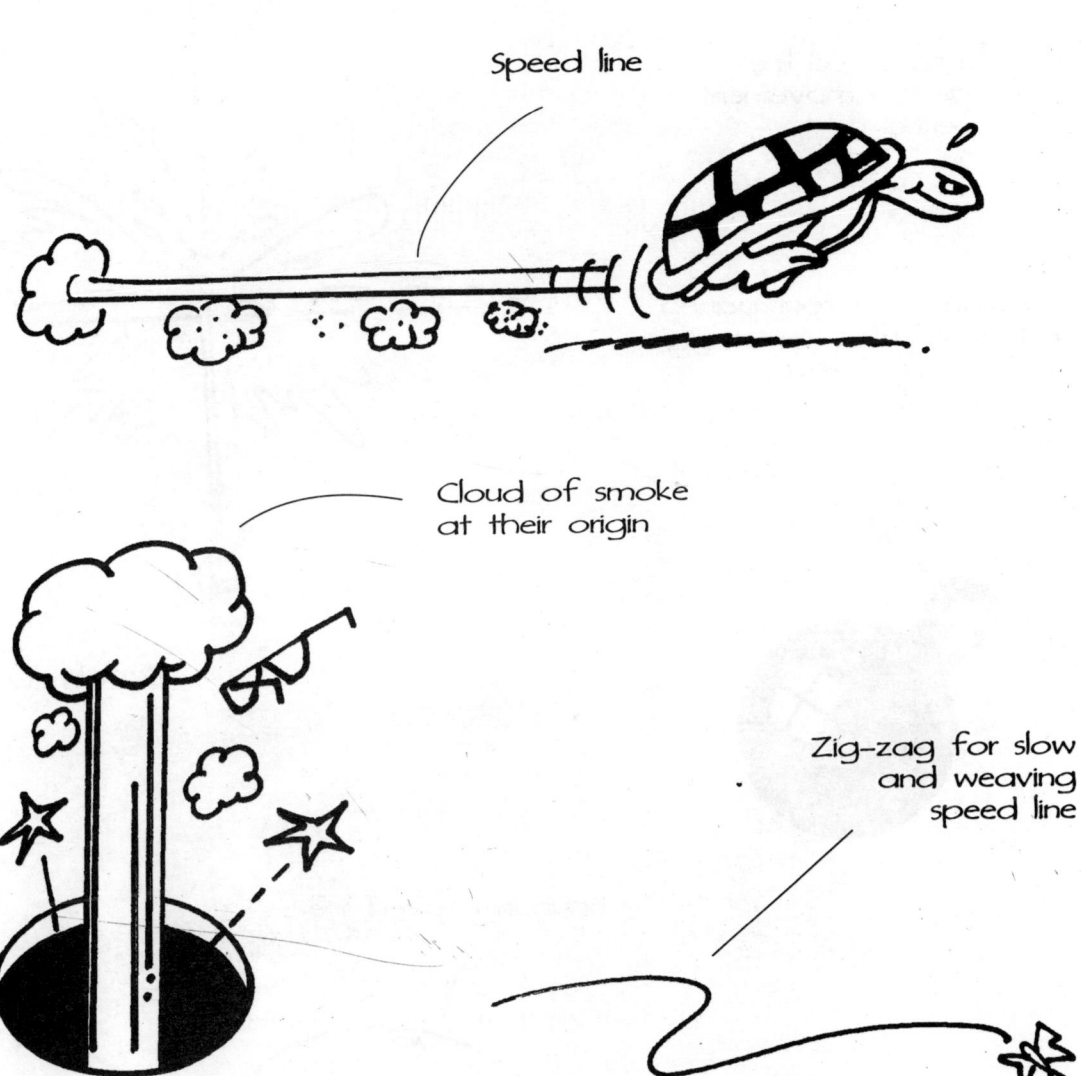

Speed line

Cloud of smoke at their origin

Zig-zag for slow and weaving speed line

Tiny repeated lines
suggest a movement
sequence.

Reflection of a four paned
window-to show something
is either new or shiny.

Water splash

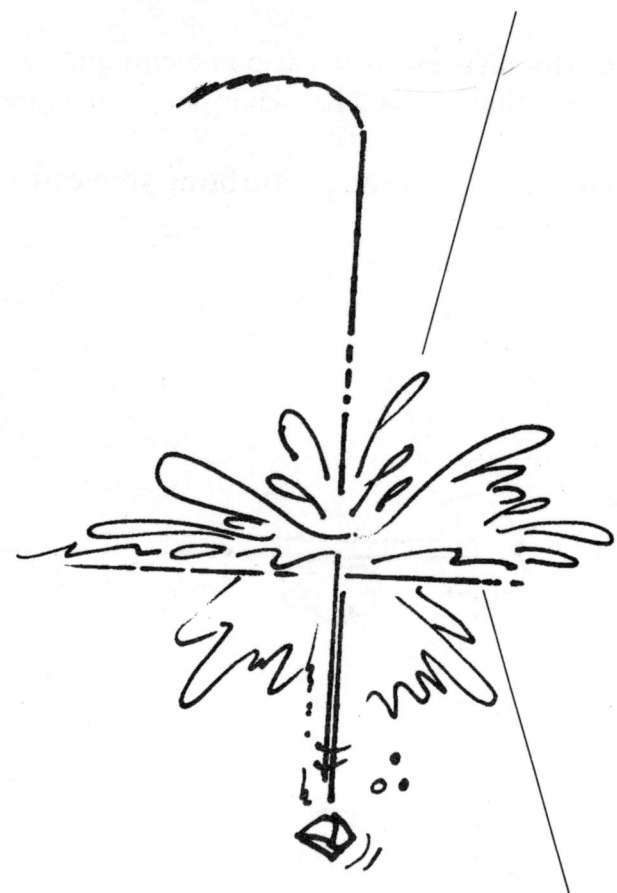

Calm water

Bouncing Speed line

A broken line puts movement
into solid images.

Speed lines in small
bunches at many places

Dust clouds

Foul language depicted with funny, creative punctuation

Little circles above the head of a drunk character

Floating sound

Radiating sweat beads for someone shown working hard or feeling very worried.

Dizziness shown with symbols of planets, stars, etc.

Light bulb popping when an idea strikes

Bull's horn to show a person thinking evil thoughts

Lines radiating around the head to suggest shock or surprise

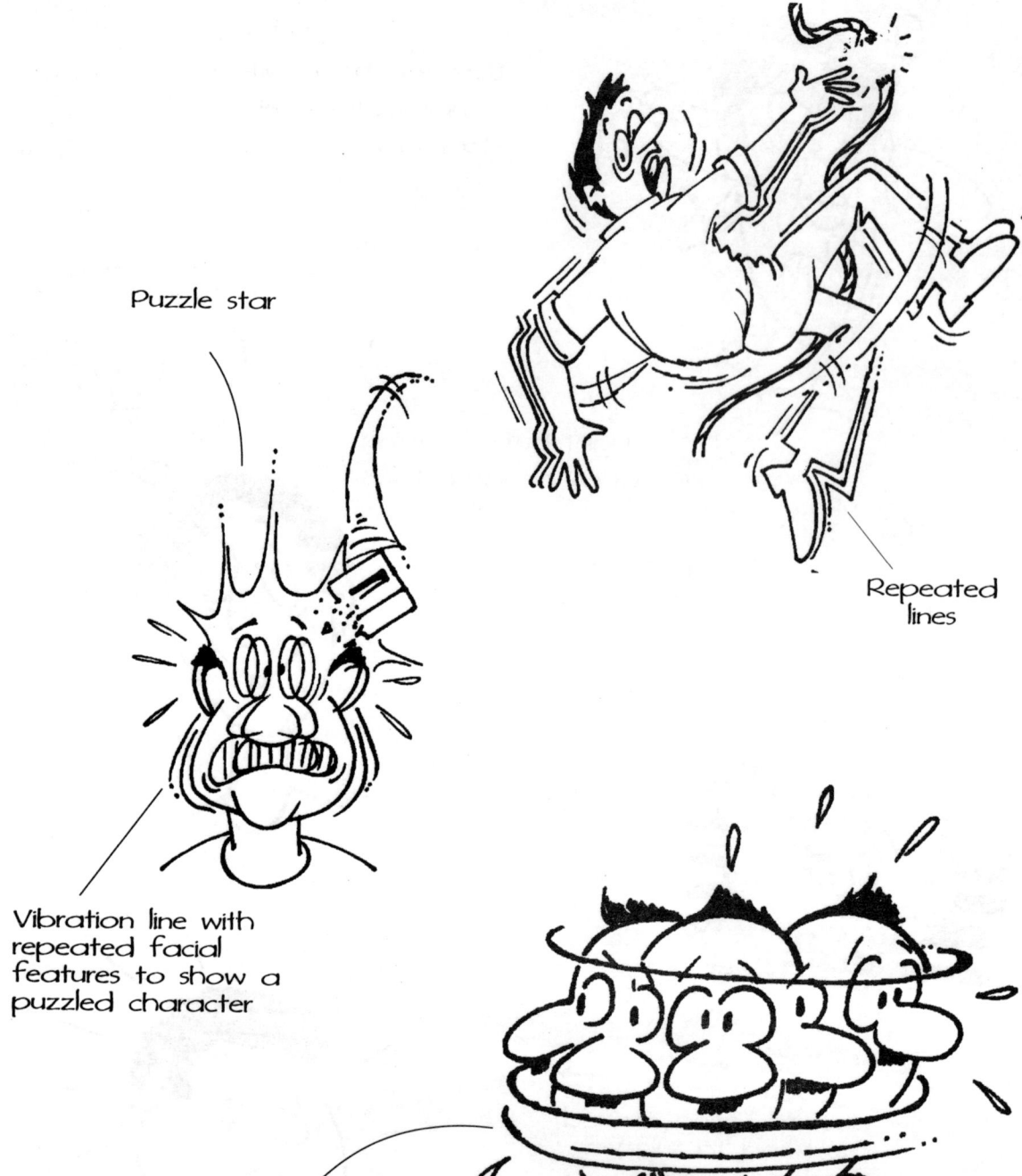

Puzzle star

Repeated
lines

Vibration line with
repeated facial
features to show a
puzzled character

Curved speed lines,
for a bewildered character standing still

Hurt stars

Impact star

Explosions

Popularly used in cartooning, these could be in the form of atomic explosions or destruction by dynamite.

Bomb

Dynamite

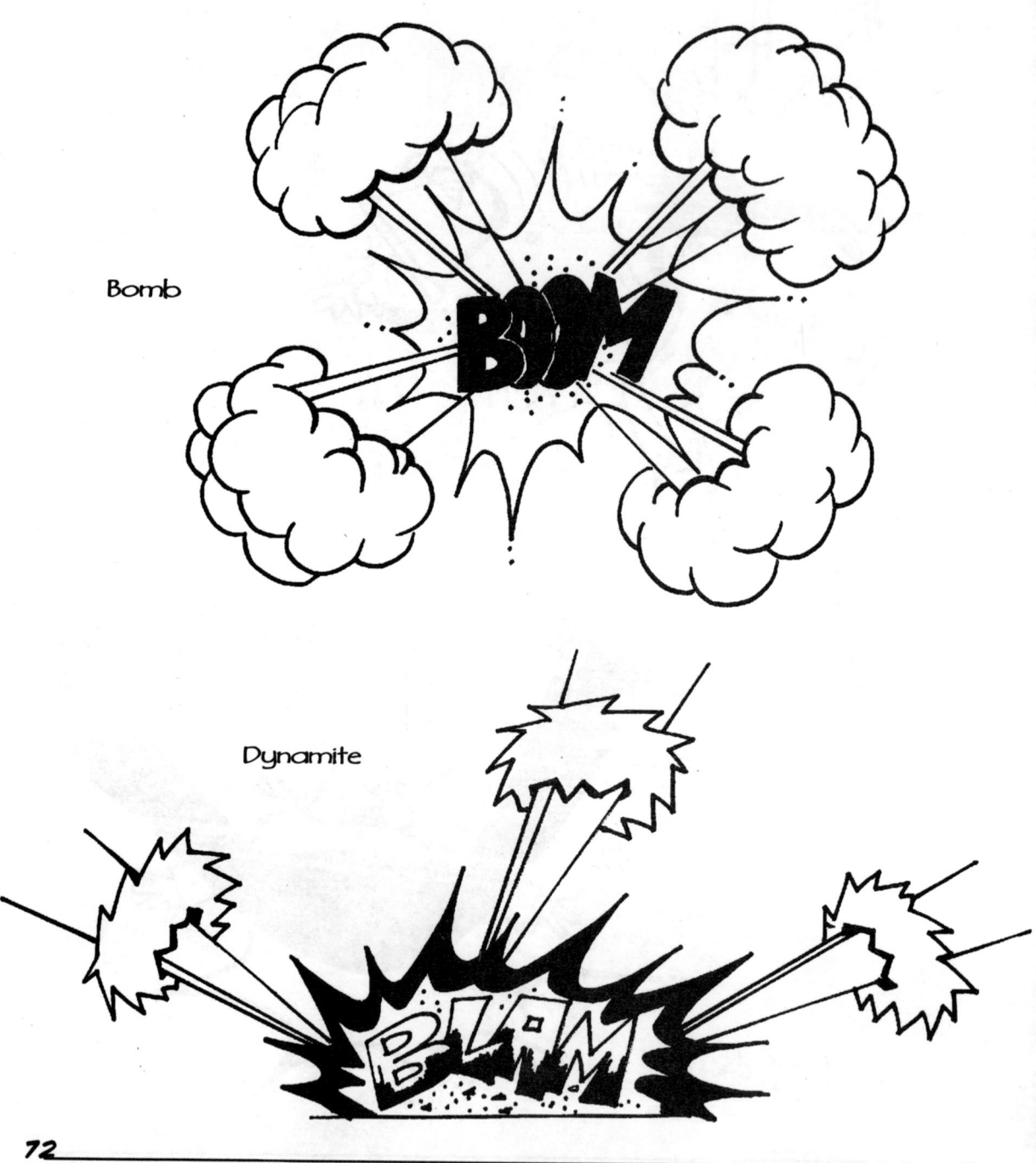

Atomic

Fight cloud

A fight scene is often hidden by a cloud with just glimpses of flying dentures, shoes, limbs, etc .The reader doesn't see anybody getting hurt.

Fight cloud

Tip: Exaggerated body language can enhance the humour in your cartoon.

CARTOON THEMES

There are four concepts which a cartoonist can modify, mix and interpret to produce ideas of her/his own. These are contrast/misleading, prop/verbal, surprise and stereotype.

You can also consider work with a partner who is good at thinking up ideas and jokes, or else, trust your own sense of humour.

Contrast and Misleading

Contrast cartoons focus on basic differences to create humour, such as tall and short, honest and corrupt, hot and cold, etc.

Misleading cartoons rely on the contrast between what you thought was about to happen and what actually happens.

Prop and Verbal

Prop cartoons use visual material which consists of unlikely combinations of items and characters to create humour .

Jargon or technical words are used in unlikely situations to create a humorous effect.

Surprise

The entertainment value of these cartoons comes from the fact that the reader or one or more characters knows something that is hidden from the main character.

This usually revolves around the character getting in or out of trouble.

Stereotype

Situations that are familiar are used in these cartoons like a doctor's waiting room, a court room, the jail, a desert or an island, etc.

Closing note

It has been fun writing and illustrating this book and I hope you are inspired to grab your paper and pencil to master the art of cartooning. Until next time ... happy tooning!

Other books by Ajit Narayan:

Cartooning with Ajit Narayan
Ajit Narayan
Simple steps that teach cartooning
techniques.

Pbk • 60 pp • b/w

How To Draw Animal Cartoons
Ajit Narayan
Handy tips from an experienced
cartoonist.

Pbk • 76 pp • b/w